# The Crane

# The Crane

Halim Barakat

Translated by
Bassam Frangieh
Roger Allen

The American University in Cairo Press
Cairo New York

First published in 2008 by
The American University in Cairo Press
113 Sharia Kasr el Aini, Cairo, Egypt
420 Fifth Avenue, New York, NY 10018
www.aucpress.com



Dar el Kutub No. 20182/07
ISBN 978 977 416 141 4

Dar el Kutub Cataloging-in-Publication Data

Barakat, Halim
The Crane / Halim Barakat; translated by Bassam Frangieh and Roger Allen.—Cairo: The American University in Cairo Press, 2008
p. cm.
ISBN 977 416 141 6
1. Arabic fiction I. Frangieh, Bassam (trans.) II. Allen, Roger (jt. trans.) III. Title
813

1 2 3 4 5 6 7 8 12 11 10 09 08

Designed by Sally Boylan/AUC Press Design Center
Printed in Egypt

# Contents

This is the soil that sank its roots in my poetry.

—Pablo Neruda

Deep inside me as in that lost lake
there dwells the vision of a bird.

—Pablo Neruda

Come, my darling, and take a look
Halim Barakat is an open book.

# Death of the Crane

Suddenly in the Kafrun sky a flock of cranes appeared, creating a tremendous commotion. Proudly they soared, harbingers of autumn after a long, hot summer and seasons rich with grape, fig, and pomegranate.

We ran barefoot, watching them intently, fascinated by their flight patterns, their huge wings and long necks. On they came, flock after flock in awesome procession, their formations drawing black lines in the space between the clear blue sky and the trees reflected in the river.

Right at the front was a V-shaped flock led by an enormous crane; from it two lines branched out on either side while other flocks followed from various directions: the springs at Karkar, Shaykh Hasan, and al-Sheer.

The V-shapes were transformed into circles as they hovered over the river and al-Sayida and al-Sa'ih, two mountains looking down on a lush valley as deep as an ancient wound and tilting a little toward each other as though engaged in a scolding match or else thinking about it.

The cranes had their huge black wings fully extended, revealing their white breasts. They glided through the air like clouds, plunged like thunderbolts, soared like gods, then hovered relentlessly over a single spot like the sun. Up they climbed and soared, down they dived and plunged.

We watched enthralled as they took control of a sky that was cloudless but for a few white wisps as delicate as scarves. The cranes soared freely through the vast expanse, bewitched by its transparency and nakedness, like a girl gazing at her breasts reflected in the water. As if oblivious to hunger and thirst, they kept up their game, heedless of the hunters below who had left their homes carrying rusty rifles and headed for the rooftops or up into the hills.

Even after all these long, tiring years, the sound of those shots still echoes in my mind. One after another they came, just like frantic heartbeats. They kept booming on and on in every direction, sounding like the outbreak of war after a prolonged era of tedious peace.

Now everything changes. In a flash, flight patterns are transformed into a scene of chaos; the circles disintegrate as though blown outward by an explosion. Like heartbeats, wings flap in panic. The sky itself is transformed as the clear, calm, blue expanse is stained by puffs of gray smoke where shots have been fired.

The panicked cranes scatter, each one flying off in a different direction and emitting piercing screams. Some plunge to their inevitable death in valleys as deep as the heart's own sorrows. Their feathers flutter through the air and float slowly to the ground.

I can still vividly recall it all even today; I always will, no doubt. I can clearly remember the anguished cries, but I have no idea how to describe the scene, even if it is just to myself in rare moments of composure. Those cries blend with an image of black and white feathers floating through the air, dropping slowly to the ground as though intent on playing some innocent game in spite of the imminent catastrophe.

Like a thunderbolt a crane came crashing to earth right in front of me; at that moment I was standing under Eagle's Nest by the smooth rock of 'al-Dahr.' It lay there writhing on the ground, letting out piercing screams that blended pain, outrage, and terror. I rushed over, intending to pick it up, but fear held me back. I was scared of it and upset by its fate. I moved toward it gingerly, hoping not to scare it too much, but it started writhing and screaming even more, so I moved away. I tried again, moving forward cautiously and gently extending my hand. How could I convince it I was not a hunter? I couldn't blame it for not trusting me. Ignoring my fear I went over and bent over it. By now, it was calming down a bit. I managed to give its long neck a gentle rub with my hand. It still did not trust me, nor did I feel safe as I looked at that hard, red beak. Even so, I realized I had to pluck up courage.

Its right wing was obviously broken. Blood was oozing out, staining its black and white feathers a vivid crimson. It needed help, but I had no idea how to treat it. I was worried that, instead of helping it, I might actually do it even more harm. I couldn't stop trembling.

At that crucial moment, Raif came rushing up like some ravenous tiger that has picked up the scent of blood. Before I was even aware of what was happening, he had snatched the wounded crane and ran quickly down to the river where he proudly displayed it to anyone he met. When the crowd of inquisitive onlookers got too large, he pushed his way through and ran off, just in case they tried to snatch the crane away from him as he had done from me.

Later on, I discovered that Raif had slaughtered the crane; he had skinned and barbecued it, then eaten it. It was only much later that he admitted to me that the meat was tough and bitter. But he had no regrets. He had sold its long legs to a man who used them to make cigarette holders for wealthy smokers.

# The Old Shaykh

My mother holds Mona's hand gently. Mona was born in America and does not know any Arabic. My mother smoothes Mona's little palm in her own as she sings:

*Soft, O how soft, are your hands, O Mona;*
*How lovely and soft they are.*

Mona enjoys this delightful game. She stares at us, demanding an explanation of my mother's rhymes. My mother points to the middle of the child's palm and rubs her fingers over the criss-cross lines:

"Here's a water fountain where a bird comes to drink."

She holds the child's fingers one by one, beginning with the index finger.

"This finger picks up the bird. The middle finger slaughters it. The ring finger skins it. The little finger barbecues it. And this old shaykh (here she grabs Mona's thumb and adopts a histrionic tone), he eats a lot."

Slowly, very slowly, my mother's fingers crawl ant-like up Mona's arm, then suddenly dash up to her shoulder. Again she toys with her voice:

*Crawl, crawl, baby, crawl*
*Take this coin to market*
*And buy some candies*
*To sweeten your tooth.*

Suddenly my mother tickles her under the arms; the little girl laughs from the depths of her heart, even though she doesn't understand any Arabic. Had she understood, she might well have not laughed; she's very fond of birds. Once again, she looks at us, asking for an explanation, but I ignore her request. I don't want to shock her by telling her how the thirsty bird that comes to drink from the lake of that soft hand is so cruelly slaughtered.

# Changing into a Tree Trunk

Dear crane, I have yet to learn your language. I have not learned it from your screams, but maybe I will from your silence, your broken wing, and your feathers floating through the air. I cannot understand your enigmatic language, but I still think I know you. A long time ago you were born in my dreams and were shot down in my nightmares; I have often heard you speaking in the languages of anguish, hunger, and lust. You left me to ponder your death in my eternal loneliness. Yes, I am that child from Kafrun, companion of springs, pomegranates, rocks, and willows reflected in the river and dwelling in my unconscious.

Crane is what I call you, but what do you call yourself? Do you have another name besides the one we've given you? What is your relationship to your name? Let's exchange names if you like. Give me your wings, and I'll give you my home. Does the sky's nakedness seduce you the way my beloved's does me? Why do your wounds still haunt me?

Over forty years later you emerge from the depths of my memory as though roused from an invisible world buried deep inside me. Why now? I don't know. True, my beloved and I were watching a bluebird bathe in a small birdbath we had made in our yard. No sooner did it fly up into our neighbor's tree than I plunged deep into recesses of memory, chasing strange associations that washed over me like waves upon the Sandbridge shores.

For a while I am floating on waves.

"Why are you looking at me like that?" my beloved asks.

"In you I can see my own self," I respond at once with a certain amount of obfuscation.

She is obviously not convinced. "I didn't realize I was a mirror," she comments dryly with a shake of her head.

I pick up on her mood. "I envision myself as a tree trunk in your lovely cheeks."

With that her indifference changes to sarcasm. "You mean, an aged tree trunk transformed into an anthill."

"No," I retort, "a sprouting willow-branch."

All too familiar with the strange associations I make, she made no reply, but looked away, obviously thinking I was talking nonsense. I stared hard at her, but she continued to ignore me.

She too retreated now into her inner self. Her expression relaxed like a clear sky on an autumn day. I longed to know what was going through her mind; were flocks of cranes crossing her sky too, I wondered? The way I saw it, she was avoiding my glances so as to keep her own distance; so deep had she plunged into her own thoughts that I'd almost disappeared from her world.

There being nothing else to do, I returned to my own private musings. This may have been the first time we had had a really prolonged crisis in our relationship. Previously I hadn't taken her complaints seriously even though they were far more than fleeting moments of anger. No, I didn't take them seriously enough because there wasn't much I could do to change our situation. But this time she really meant it.

"Listen," she said, "I'm fed up with living like this, working, sleeping, reading the newspaper, watching TV, paying bills, inviting people, cooking, and washing dishes. How long do you plan to live like this? What does it all mean? When are we going to enjoy what we have? Tomorrow we may not have anything, not even our own lives. Just look at your mother. What does she have left? Is there anything more precious than the mind? She can't control her mind or body any more. Why do you argue with her and upset yourself? You forget that she's eighty-seven; she's not going to change her habits now. Forget it! Arguments, shouting, getting upset, and then guilt-feelings. I'm fed up with it all! Do something about it."

Right then I knew she was right, but had no clue what to do about it. I couldn't accept the truth that my mother had become senile. I always expected her to be capable of using her mind, but she no longer had one to use. It had escaped from her personal control and was now meandering hither and thither in a vast firmament of confusion.

I did nothing. Until recently I had thought that my beloved and I could overcome any crisis merely because we loved each other, so we had ignored our daily problems till they reached a breaking point. Needless to say, I assumed we would overcome these problems and start again. I dreamed of being liberated from all our responsibilities, including our jobs and the need to travel all over the world. But we never do anything worth mentioning. We get up in the morning, drink coffee, read the paper, go to work, and lose ourselves in its petty details. We come home exhausted, so we have a drink, eat, watch television, and fall asleep in our chairs before going to bed. Recently I have started playing backgammon, even though I always used to scoff at it and all other types of vacuous entertainment. I have also found myself writing to a friend in Kafrun, asking him to send me a mankala like the one we used to play on when we were kids. He wrote back that no one plays it any more; the younger generation has never even heard of it. My beloved noticed these changes in my life.

"You're going back to your roots," she remarked, "playing backgammon and carrying worry-beads. Now you want to play mankala. Next thing you'll be smoking a waterpipe and wearing a sirwal!"

We've been married twenty-six years; in a few months we'll be celebrating yet another anniversary. I wonder, will we have a party? How many times have we thought about celebrating our silver wedding anniversary, but have always found ourselves too busy with other things?

"No surprises," I told myself. "I'd better share my idea with her, then we can plan things together."

After discussing things, we finally decided to have a simple, modest celebration, just like our wedding to which we had only invited a few relatives. Every year we had spent wonderful vacations traveling to different parts of the world, but they were all short. We always came back to pick up our old routine and follow news about our country's death, a process as slow as my mother's. Yet more tragedies, more disintegration (for man will always turn on himself if he can't find anyone else to fight); more futile conflict; more historic defeats; and yet more downward slides to levels of pure farce that none of us could even have conceived of reaching.

Eventually our problems did not disappear; in fact, they got much worse. One night, after we had gone to bed, my mother got up and starting wandering around the house. We don't know why, but she went downstairs into the basement without turning the light on. She fell down several steps, hit her head against the wall and the iron railing, and slumped to the floor. We heard the thumps and came charging downstairs to find out what had happened. She lay motionless at the bottom of the stairs, her tiny body lying in a pile over her head. She was breathing fitfully. I was in a panic, as panicked as I had been with the wounded crane. I had no idea what to do. I carried my mother up to her bed, while my beloved called the ambulance, which came and took her to the hospital. We followed and sat in the emergency room, waiting for the doctor. It was a long wait. As my mother became more and more agitated, so did we. When the doctor finally arrived, they took her to the x-ray room. Once again it was a long wait: past midnight, then 1:00 a.m., then 1:30 a.m. At last, the doctor returned to tell us that she had certainly broken her arm and wrist, and the heavy blows to her head might have caused serious damage.

All night I stretched out on a chair next to her bed. She was completely delirious. The nurse gave her a sedative and secured her to the bed so she wouldn't fall out. Days and nights passed. The doctor told us that all he could do is put her broken arm in a cast. He added that she may go on living like this for years or die at any moment.

Since then, she has been living in a nebulous state somewhere between consciousness and unconsciousness, life and death. Sometimes she is in a coma, at other times, half-awake, alternating between silence and utter confusion, clinging to life while yearning to return to dust. She doesn't realize what has happened to her, where she is, and who we are. We have been erased from her consciousness. Instead she now dominates ours. She calls out various names from the distant past that are dear to her. As the present vanishes, so the past reawakens. She names her sisters, Latifa, Nazira, and Nada; her uncle Rashid; her aunt Kulthum; her cousins Khishfa and Barbara; and her childhood friend Fidda.

There was one moment when I had the happy feeling that she might be regaining her consciousness. I heard her asking God loudly why her mother had died before she had even come to know her, why her husband had died young, and why He kept refusing to take her soul and relieve her suffering. I asked her who she was.

"Halim's mother," she replied.

I was thrilled. "Who am I?" I asked.

"You're Halim, my heart's own darling."

"And you're mine too," I answered.

With that I kissed her head, her face, and her hand. "Good for you, Mother," I kept saying, "That's wonderful!" Reassured now that I had not been completely erased from her consciousness, I gave her a piece of candy.

"And who am I?" my beloved asked her.

She smiled but said nothing for a while. She seemed to be recognizing her but could not come up with her name. My beloved asked the question again.

"You are the priceless gift," my mother replied. "You come from a good family."

"Fine! What's my name?"

"Your name? Your name? Oh my God, I have forgotten! Your name is God's dew."

Now it was my brother's turn. "Who am I?" he asked.

"You know who you are," she said "Why are you asking?"

We all laugh, grieve, cry, and smile. I find myself confronting God face to face.

"O God," I say, "listen! I need to know Your intentions. Why are You torturing her? Why her? Have You forgotten how many times she prayed to You every day, how many candles she lit, how much incense she burned, and how many solemn vows she made! She wouldn't dare ask such questions herself; she would consider it heresy. But why should she be scared to ask? Why are You punishing her? Why such cruelty? She doesn't deserve it. I do not think she's committed any more sins than Your prophets. Why, oh God? How many times has she implored You from the bottom of her heart: 'Oh God, I beg You, let me rest in peace! Please honor my old age.'

"Oh God, are You still alive? When were You born? How many million light years separate You from human beings? Were

You born before or after the birth of mankind? Who created whom? Why did my father die so suddenly in the prime of his youth, and yet my mother lingers here in a slow death that never comes? Are You using his death and her life to chastise me? Are You using her to punish me? Why? I don't understand; I want to understand, but I don't. You might as well answer because I will keep asking my questions. How much longer are You going to be evasive? How many light years are You from mankind? Why don't You pity her and let her die? She believes in You completely; she is devoutly faithful. She has toiled diligently in Your pastures. She has denied herself and been the most noble of mothers. She says that You put those who fear You to the test. Why?"

I don't expect God to answer, so I turn to the doctor: "Medicine has made many advances, so now you can delay her death for a long time without ever curing her. It won't cure her or let her die in peace. Why are you prescribing a treatment that won't cure her? Why are you keeping her in this endless state of nothingness between life and death?"

God provides no answer, but the doctor does. He agrees with my diagnosis of the situation and acknowledges that there's nothing he can do. I acknowledge my sense of helplessness too, and God concedes His by remaining silent and aloof. Her slow, lingering death is prolonged; it stretches out like a shadow at sunset, turning into a gigantic phantom that envelops the world in its dark shadow. When will sunset come? When is redemption to be?

The more questions I ask, the more vague things become. The more she erases me from her consciousness, the more she dominates my own. The weaker she becomes, the more I love her and link myself to her. It is with her that I stay up at night and wake up in the early morning.

As soon as I stop confronting God and medicine, the god of this sick age, I realize that my unvoiced distress has another cause. As I leave the hospital and walk along the riverbank, my imagination is invaded by pictures from a documentary film I watched the night before. Herds of wild bulls and cows are grazing freely in vast open fields, tilting at each other with large pointed horns, mating shamelessly in the open air, effortlessly chewing grass and tree branches, and stretching out lazily in the shade. All of a sudden a pack of wolves attacks the herd and chases a small calf. Its mother is the only one to rush to defend it. The rest of the herd retreats to a safe place and watches the chase, raising their ears and tails in the open air. The mother defends her calf heroically; several times she manages to disperse the wolf pack all on her own. But the wolves have a clear strategy; time and again they restart the chase. The task is subdivided: some attack the mother to keep her away, while others go after the calf. The battle intensifies. The big bulls stay out of the fight, simply standing there watching with bewildered expressions. Finally the calf falls prey to the wolves. The mother bellows her despair, then without looking back rejoins the rest of the herd.

Now I confront the Arabs as I have done the doctor and God. Palestine falls prey. Beirut is in ruins. Basra is threatened with ruin. Southern Lebanon is occupied. Why is it only the mother who fights back? You Arab leaders, you're just a herd of bulls. You too raise your horns and look bewildered; you cringe in fear as you watch; you tilt at one another, secretly mating in corridors, devouring everything within reach, lolling like lazy idiots beyond the reach of history.

What is the point of confrontation? Ah, what a tragicomedy!

# Journey on a Flying Carpet over a Thickly Colored Forest

After a hot summer, Washington had been transformed into a dense forest of brilliant, undulating, blending colors. It was a wonderful autumn day, just like the one when I had watched the crane plunge to the ground in Kafrun. Instead of using the time to take a vacation with my beloved and wash away all the anxieties that were pent up inside us like a black cloud, I was going away on a trip to take part in a conference.

I called an airline reservation office several times before a tired woman's voice answered, "This is Kathy, can I help you?"

"Yes, Kathy, I want to book a seat for New York City."

No sooner had she asked me for my name, travel dates, and other information required in such cases than she asked me, "You have an accent. Where are you from?"

"I am an Arab from Syria."

Her tone of voice changed completely. "Really? I thought so—I'm half Syrian. Just imagine. I only found out about my Syrian identity when I was twenty-seven. I discovered I'd been adopted. My real mother was Syrian, and my father was Greek. I wish you'd tell me about Syria."

"We'd need to meet. When did you discover you were Syrian?"

"You're an Arab all right. You really want to know how old I am."

"No, no. I wanted to know how long you've be trying to discover your origins."

"I didn't try very hard. I don't know many Arabs and don't have time to read. Tell me, are you an Arab shaykh?"

"I'm an Arab, but not a shaykh."

"Are you as handsome as Omar Sharif? Your voice is exciting."

I decided this woman was nuts, but was fascinated enough to keep talking. "No, I'm not handsome."

"I'm not pretty either. Tell me, I understand Syrians are good businessmen. I'm not a businesswoman, and I don't like business or businessmen."

"I don't like business either. I'm a village boy, and my father was a peasant—or rather, a mule-driver. Your mother probably came from a Syrian village."

Her next question came as a surprise. "Do you have a harem?"

"Things have changed a lot. The age of the harem is over. By the way, ordinary people didn't have harems."

"No, please, don't tell me you've all become westernized. Why change? I wish my mother had never come to America. If only she had stayed in Syria, I would have been born, raised, and lived in a Syrian village close to people and the soil. I would rather be a respectable woman in an Arab family than have to put up with this terrible loneliness. Here life destroys our humanity. Loneliness consumes you from within. It's not enough to have a dog. We're just machines. We eat, drink, and sleep all alone, just like machines. Why change things? You must preserve your culture."

"We're bulls too." I laugh but offer no explanation.

This woman is obviously nuts. Madness comes in many forms; her kind is a rare treat.

"Please keep on talking," she insists. "Your voice is deep, warm, and beautiful. Are you daring? Your voice is truly beautiful.

Say something. Why don't you record your voice? Thousands of women would love to hear a voice like yours. Make a record. You'd sell thousands of copies. You'd get rich, return to Syria, and bring back the days of the harem. If you like, I'd join your harem."

It was at this point that I realized things had gone beyond the bounds of rationality and irrationality. I considered thanking her and ending the conversation. Instead I found myself asking her, "What about getting together?"

"No, no," she replied. "My whole life has been a series of disappointments. I can do without any more. I used to imagine I was a certain kind of person, only to discover at the age of twenty-seven that I was someone else. I don't expect you to be as charming as your voice. This doesn't bother me much. What I'm afraid of is dashing your hopes. Forgive me. Let's change the subject. What sort of work do you do?"

"I'm a novelist."

"Wow, I'm talking to a writer? I've never spoken to a writer in my life. I can't believe it! Syrian and a writer! You're all I could long for. What do you write?"

"I don't know how to answer such a question. What do you mean?"

"Do you write modern or traditional literature?"

"Modern, I suppose."

"No, no! You've disappointed me. I don't like modern literature. I prefer older literature. Modern writers must be as crazy as their writings."

"Well, don't forget that we live in a crazy age."

"True. Have a nice trip," she said and hung up the phone.

I forgot to ask her if she had made reservations for me on the flying carpet. I thought of calling her again, but I decided to put her charming manner aside as a vague question. I was convinced she wasn't being sarcastic or frivolous, but she wasn't serious either. Maybe she was being sarcastic, or then again maybe for the first time ever I'm actually going to travel on the flying carpet.

I reminded my beloved of the encounter. Once again she assured me the woman was being serious. "You know," she went on, "that of all things it is comedies, legends, and dreams that are among the truest and most serious. How often did you keep saying that when you were reading Freud?"

"It's an enduring truth, no doubt about it."

Actually I loathe the expression 'no doubt about it,' but I said it nonetheless. "I've often listened to tales," I added by way of explanation, "that I was firmly convinced could never actually happen; until, that is, they actually happened to me. The story of Jonah entering the whale's belly, for example, and his subsequent emergence from it. I considered that to be a mere fable, but that was before I entered the belly of a beast far more terrible than any whale—New York City."

# The Labyrinth of the System

The doors of the airplane were being closed, so I fastened my seatbelt and slumped in my seat. After a prolonged period of turmoil and anticipation I could relax a bit. I was especially pleased the airplane was leaving on time, so I would not miss my flight from New York to Madrid and then to Casablanca, where I was going to participate in a conference that had already begun.

The airplane rolled slowly down the runway, but before long it moved to one side and came to a stop. When passengers started asking questions, the captain tersely explained that the New York area had been hit by a violent rainstorm and they had decided to wait it out here.

In considerable panic I summoned the stewardess and told her that, in view of the situation, I preferred to discontinue my journey since I was obviously going to miss my flight to Madrid. She informed me that it was not possible to disembark. She tried to calm me down by pointing out that all flights would be delayed; they would be able to reschedule my departure in the event my connecting flight left prior to my arrival.

Once again I slumped back in my seat, but found it impossible to control my visible anxiety. All I could do, I realized, was to surrender my fate to the machine. I decided to have a drink, read, and listen to music, come what may. I tried in vain to convince myself that "I am constantly changing," as opposed to Arabs who say, "I am what I was" and Americans who claim, "I am what I am." For my part I'm with the Italians who sing, "Whatever will be will be."

I ask for a glass of whiskey, but what arrives is more like water. I listen to music, but it does nothing to calm my nerves. I try to read, but nothing sinks in. Then I notice that an old woman is asking if she can take the seat next to me. I stand up for her, respectful but somewhat put out. "Sorry to disappoint you!" she says, having some fun at my expense before settling in her seat. "I'm sure you'd rather have a pretty girl sitting next to you, not some ugly old crone."

At a loss for words I had to laugh. I went back to writing some notes.

"Is that Hebrew you're writing?" she asked looking at the script.

"No, Arabic."

Her expression changed, as though she had just been faced with a shocking reality. Somewhat hesitantly she told me she had just attended a meeting at the White House where she was awarded a medal for her tireless fundraising efforts for Israel. Despite my obvious dismay she kept talking. For a moment I had the idea, just out of spite, of telling her that I was a member of the Popular Front for the Liberation of Palestine, but fortunately my better judgment prevailed. A confrontation would have served no purpose. I withdrew, tortoise-like, into my inner world and waited for the plane to move. This machine had swallowed me down its belly and was now refusing to disgorge me, so I surrendered my destiny to it.

In order to put an end to the conversation, I put on the earphones and looked for a classical music channel. I was thrilled to realize that what I was listening to was Richard Wagner's opera "The Ring."

"Do you like Wagner?" I asked my neighbor, removing the earphones.

"I hate him."

"Why?"

"Because he's a Nazi."

"Do you know when he lived?"

"It doesn't matter."

"Yes, it does matter. He died in 1883, six years before Hitler was born. Wagner dreamed of establishing a socialist society. People say that, when he was conductor of the Royal Opera, he was bold enough to confront the King of Saxony and ask him to stand by the exploited working classes. What was the result? The king exiled Wagner for a prolonged period, during which the latter wrote pamphlets about art and revolution, as well as the libretto for the 'The Ring.'"

At this point I noticed she had put her own earphones on, so I gave up; she was probably listening to Frank Sinatra. I ignored her and went back to listening to Wagner, captivated by the bitter struggle between love and the lust for power. I realize full well that man bears the responsibility for the salvation of the gods as well as for their creation. God will not save my mother until I free her from His power over her fate. Would I rescue Him through my mother's death? You believers who have inherited your faith just like your names, language, and gender, tell me, who rescues whom? Contrary to your beliefs, it is gods who sin and Man alone who can save them. Richard Wagner, I completely agree with you: Erda, the Earth Mother, is the source of wisdom. The artist lives by his works. His death is the life of his work. But what then is the meaning of non-life and non-death?

After the second drink (and without my neighbor hearing me), I asked Wagner, "Have you ever seen the crane? Have you seen how it gets shot? If you had, it would have inspired your greatest music. I know you haven't. Who among creative artists has ever given his utmost? So let me tell you something about the crane; I'm sure you'd be interested to hear something. You love powerful symbols. It has a close relationship with the wind; its huge wings are sails to navigate the sky-sea. Its neck is like a bridge between two islands, large, proud, assertive, tranquil amid storms, continually migrating between the south and the north (and the dangers lurking in each), driven by thirst, hunger, lust, and warmth. One world traversed, another reveals itself. It has a history of relationships with vast distances and horizons that open to horizons even broader than its own vision. It also has a history of relationships with man. It has known man as a skillful hunter and had thus been raised to be wary of him. Yet caution has not much diminished its unquenchable desire for adventure and constant migration between the earth's different climates."

I realized that I was talking to Wagner instead of listening to his music, so I listened instead. But once again my imagination transported me to other worlds. After an hour-and-a-half delay—with me a captive of my imagination, the captain announced that the storm was almost over and we would be on our way in a matter of minutes. The plane deposited me in New York, only for me to discover that my other flight had already left. They tried in vain to rearrange my flight schedule and reclaim my luggage, but I realized that the machine was not done with me yet and that I was actually involved in the workings of a larger machine. I complain to the managers, but only after standing in long lines before reaching them. I discover that they too are mere cogs in the mighty machine. None of them was prepared to take any responsibility or even to discuss my problem; it was beyond their limited realm of expertise. Everyone was simultaneously responsible and not responsible. No one could do anything to correct the mistake.

I ran through the labyrinth of this dreadful system, alone, bewildered, anxious, and angry. I slowed down, well aware that all I could do was wait until the machine chose to spit me out, my core essence disfigured. As I waited, I suddenly discovered that I'd lost my money. With that, I went completely crazy. I searched frantically through my pockets over and over again, but found nothing. Had I dropped it somewhere? Where? Had someone picked my pockets without my even being aware of it?

With that I phoned Maya and asked her to put me up for the night. She came out to the airport as fast as she could and rescued my disfigured form from the jaws of the machine-beast. After driving my fractured self to her apartment, she proceeded to reassemble me bit by bit. We drank, dined, and listened to Indian music, while she told me of her experiences inside the marriage machine. She had entered it in a drunken state and now kept charging through its labyrinth in quest of an exit or entrance. During our conversation I kept remembering her as a young girl, full of life, happy, and dancing barefoot at lively parties.

Just then the thought occurred to me that the person who had robbed me of my money had called his girlfriend, invited her out to a fancy restaurant and dance hall, and then slept with her in a first-class hotel—all at my expense. The very idea which hit me like lightning on a dark night made me roar with laughter, so much so in fact that I couldn't stop. I shared the thought with Maya.

"What's important," she replied, "is that you escaped from the belly of the whale, Jonah of Kafrun."

"We only emerge from one whale to enter another."

"So who's the pessimist, you or I?"

"Neither you nor I! It's the system itself that's rotten."

"More coffee?"

"Half a cup, please. You make good coffee."

The next day, I strolled down Fifth Avenue between the Village and Central Park, looking at people and store windows.

I kept trying to rid myself of all the tensions the system had roused, as though unraveling threads entwined around my inner self.

As I was walking, I suddenly noticed a black man coming straight toward me. I tried to get out of his way, but he stuck his finger out at me. "You!"

I stopped, not knowing what to say or do. He came closer. "Jewish?" he asked.

"No."

"Italian?"

"No."

With that he gave a smile. "Al-salaamu alaykum!" he said in Arabic.

I felt an enormous sense of relief. Now I realized I was ready to go back to the airport. The return trip to Washington was on a small propeller plane. At several points during the flight I felt sure the storm was going to break it apart. I got out my notebook and wrote: "After twenty-four hours full of surprises, it wouldn't shock me now if something else happened, death included."

When I eventually exited the belly of the plane, I found myself wishing that the crazy lady had actually reserved me a seat on a flying carpet.

# The Colorful City

As the storm came to an end, once again the sun's rays bathed the colorful foliage in their fervent embrace. Trees swayed and intertwined, exulting in themselves and the entire world.

But the storm that was raging inside me had not yet subsided. At that very moment my brother arrived unexpectedly. He suggested that we go out and he would stay with our sick mother. We accepted his offer without the slightest hesitation. As we strolled along the bank of the Potomac River in Washington, for some reason I found myself recalling the day we had flown from Beirut to the United States. All of a sudden, there loomed before my eyes the mountains of Lebanon, apparently poised to leap into the sea. Small ships were plowing their way across the blue expanse of the Mediterranean; Cyprus reaching out in different directions toward Greece, Turkey, and Syria, striving to transcend its lonely courtship with the waves; fabled islands where Ulysses and Cadmus lost their way, bewitched by the siren songs of sea-nymphs. The craggy Alps untie their snowy sash to stand naked in the presence of Hannibal's ghost. Europe's green lands are an abstract painting. White clouds scurry by without pause, like herds of lambs grazed in unfenced meadows over the

Atlantic Ocean. America, land of thick forests, pierced by mighty rivers.

The plane transporting my beloved and me to America was chasing the sun, but kept its distance. Awake before sunrise in Beirut, we raced to stay ahead, but it gradually caught up with us, paralleling our progress with its brightness. Then, without ever taking its eyes off us, it moved on ahead and managed to lay down its head in sleepless New York before we had even arrived. For a long time we thought the sun was never going to set (actually it was the longest encounter with the sun I have ever had in my life). The whole airport was crowded and brightly lit, and yet, even in the midst of such a horde of arrivals, my new wife and I still managed to flirt.

So here I was, taking a first big step toward a brand new destiny, as husband and immigrant. Without planning or foresight I had left both bachelorhood and country behind. Once in a while I was gripped by a strange feeling of delight, albeit accompanied by a good deal of anxiety as well. It was only a month before the trip that we had married, and the honeymoon seemed to have only just started. We plunged straight into a new way of life. For me, travel or rather emigration to America only served to intensify my feelings. In fact I never felt I had really emigrated. The commitment that I felt to my home country was very deep, and there was no chance that I could be uprooted. As for my beloved, she was returning to her family who had emigrated long ago and made America their new home.

As we began our descent through thick white clouds over America, I recalled a time in my childhood when I had entered a patch of thick black clouds that were being illuminated by lightning flashes. My father had died suddenly in his thirties, and about the only inheritance he had left us was a mule that he'd used for transporting goods and a stone house with a dirt roof. After struggling for a year or more in the village, my mother was forced to take me, my sister, and my brother to Beirut. In the village she had worked as a baker at the clay oven (where her pay took the form of a few loaves). She had also been a seasonal harvester in remote regions that villagers called "the East." My mouth still waters when I recall those hot loaves of bread emerging from the clay ovens; that was especially so when, after my father's death, we sometimes had to eat poor people's bread that was made from a mixture of wheat, corn, and barley. After crushing an onion with shanklish, we would divide up the bread and dip the pieces in olive oil. Nowadays, even when I've eaten a large meal, the very thought of shanklish, onion, and olive oil still makes me hungry.

Times may have been hard, but we still managed to value and enjoy our way of life. We appreciated the village's beauty and its wonderful people, and were glad to have escaped the death that had snatched away four of my brothers and sisters before they were two or three years old. My father had died too, carried off without warning just when my mother was recovering from a recurrent illness. She had expected to be the one to die, not my father. He actually died just a few days after she had come home from hospital in Tripoli. She would often claim that my father had been the sacrifice for her own life; instead of her, he had been the one to die so that we would not be left as orphans. "The orphan who loses his father is no orphan," she would say, implying that, now that her husband had died, she would never remarry but rather devote her whole life to her children and grandchildren.

As she grew older, she began to see yet another aspect to the idea that my father had died in her stead. She envisioned herself assuming the rest of his life and living out its apparently endless torments. Every time she sought death, it seemed so terribly far away.

It's been months now since her terrible fall. Dreams have evaporated, leaving nightmares to fill the void. The doctor is still saying she could die at any time but might also stay in her current state for weeks, months, or even years. Once again I wonder how many times she has pleaded with her Lord, "Take me to my grave the moment I become helpless." And yet He seems oblivious to her pleas. For her, death now seems like an act of mercy. She longs to be on her way, but He still insists that the final decision is His alone. We also control her fate. It is our decision as to what she does, and when and where she does it. During her illness we have come to love her more than we did when she was strong. On the other hand, she controls our lives too. She needs constant care. Can we be reconciled, we ask ourselves, to this bitter reality? How can we deal with her dramatic shifts in mood, from deepest silence to outright confusion? For a human being, I tell myself, the most important thing to learn is when, how, and why one dies. Do I know how I am going to die, or when I want to die? When it's time to go, will I have the necessary dignity, assurance, and elegance to realize it? Will I manage to make a decision before crossing the divide that separates reality from illusion?

She transcends her suffering through song and prayer, they being perhaps the only bridges in her life that link reality and illusion. I can't sing and know nothing about praying. She sings a verse of folk poetry:

*But for patience and simile,*
*I would have gone mad long ago*
*And sought the companionship of wild beasts.*

Simile, I realize, is poetry; it's her bridge between reality and imagination. No matter how hard she's struggled during her life, she feels bound to keep on fighting till her dying breath. She worked hard in the village, and then worked just as hard in Beirut. It was only when she had found a job in the city and somewhere for us to live that she sent for us; that way, we could join her without undue hardship. I was about ten years old, my sister was eight, and my brother was six. My uncle Jamil loaded some of our things on his unruly mule, and we trailed along behind him on rough, narrow roads that led to the town of Safita. Umm Yusuf, another widow who was working in Beirut, came with us. We climbed mountains and hills and descended into valleys near villages and landmarks that we had often heard of but never seen. Every time we crossed a river or, more precisely, a stream, I stripped off and plunged into the water; then, without bothering to dry myself, I put my clothes back on and carried on walking. We used to rest by ancient shrines on hilltops in the shade of trees, especially when we had to extract thorns from our bare feet. We slept in the shadow of Safita's tower, and next morning took the bus to Tripoli. There were more chickens than passengers, tied together by the dozen. When I noticed a passenger climb onto the bus carrying a baby goat with white spots on its forehead, I sprang to my feet; at first glance, I thought it was the baby goat I had raised and sold to the butcher just a few days before our departure, but it wasn't. When the goat did not recognize me, I felt very sad.

We arrived in Tripoli and got off the bus at Bab al-Tabani. I was struck by the weird and wonderful mass of people, along with all the carts, horses, donkeys, dogs, sweets, vegetables, fruits, trash, and dust. So, was this the city I had heard so much about? I heaved a sigh of relief when we climbed on to a horse-cart and made our way to Attal Square. Now the streets were broader and the shops bigger. There were trees planted in rows like guards lined up to welcome a great leader. It was the pastry shops that attracted my attention the most, but I realized that I was not permitted to express such cravings the way my younger brother did; we had no money with us. Even though I was very hungry, I didn't ask Umm Yusuf to buy us anything. I knew that she was no less poor than my mother. Even so, she must have realized what was on my mind, because she went into a store and bought us a piece of candy.

From Attal Square we took a larger, newer, and cleaner bus to Beirut. Apart from hills rising from the sea, waves coming from distant horizons and breaking on the rocks, and the Ras al-Shaqaa Tunnel, I don't recall anything significant about the trip. I do remember the Senegalese soldiers at sunset, stopping the bus at the tunnel entrance. It was the first time I had ever seen a black man. They took us all off the bus and asked for our identification cards, something I had never heard of before. Umm Yusuf explained that we were too young to have ID cards. They insisted and kept threatening to send us back where we had come from. "Where are you, Yusuf?" I asked myself. "No one in the village could beat you at weight lifting. I wish you were here with us now. You could lift this Senegalese soldier and his rifle over your head and toss him off the cliff into the sea far below. Please help us, Yusuf. I'm asking you to come to our aid now, even though, when you were young, I can remember my father teaching you a hard lesson. You had beaten up my uncle. I can still see my father now, putting his dagger in his belt and carrying a mace to the village square. Unlike you, he was no good at weight lifting, but he was fearless; blows from his mace went unchallenged. As you are well aware, village quarrels never lasted long. Other people intervened, and a reconciliation was arranged. Actually, relationships would often improve thereafter.

How I wished Yusuf was with us now! Would the Senegalese soldier dare ask him for his identity card? Now I wonder (needless to say, at the time I wasn't aware enough to ask such a question) how strong people always manage to pit the weak against each other. The forces of imperialism continue to exploit Third World peoples to each other's disadvantage. You have heard, no doubt, how the racist government of South Africa pits black people against each other. How do America and Israel manage to interfere and prolong the Iran-Iraq war? And how does the Lebanese civil war manage to go on and on?

I'm not sure that you would believe it, Yusuf, but your mother managed to convince the Senegalese soldier to allow us to continue our trip to Beirut. We arrived there late one evening in autumn 1942. That city was to become my second village. As a precaution against air-raids there was a blackout. The covert struggle between darkness and dim, blue-painted lamps had already started.

They asked us to get off the bus in a small alley off the eastern side of al-Burj Square. I heard people whispering that we were right in the middle of the red light district, but I had no idea what that meant. Even so, I found it odd to see women shamelessly showing their legs.

We had to get to al-Hamra Street in Ras Beirut, so we followed Umm Yusuf toward the train station. My sister was wearing wooden clogs that made a lot of noise in the silent, dark-tiled streets. Jokingly I told her to take them off so she wouldn't wake the whole city and get us taken away to prison by the guards. She quickly removed them and put them in a small bundle she was carrying on her head. Even today we still remind her about this incident and share a laugh about it. When the tram arrived, it took us all by surprise; it was not at all what I was expecting. Even though it made us more flustered than we already were, we still launched ourselves at it along with everyone else. Clambering aboard without hesitation, we entered its belly like Jonah and the whale. But this particular whale had its windows painted blue. As I gazed out, I thought the whole city was colored that way. As I walked around next morning, I realized that actually it was not particularly colorful. I wonder why that first impression has remained with me until today.

# The Immolation

I stare in fascination at the black elevator operator at the George Washington monument without paying the slightest attention to what she is saying. She automatically repeats the height of the monument (something I do not even register, as it does not interest me) and informs us that it is the largest stone monument in the world. I think of interrupting her routine and suggesting that from Capitol Hill the Mall looks like a huge man (like one of the fantastic creatures in the tales of *A Thousand and One Nights*) sprawled on his back with his member rising erect into the air. Needless to say, I suppress this crude thought.

For me, the black elevator operator looked just as beautiful as early mornings in Kafrun's rainy winter. I could not take my eyes off her. For a while she tried to ignore my gaze, but then she suddenly turned and stared at me with a mixture of surprise and annoyance that was only too obvious. To avoid embarrassment I quickly looked away and instead stared at a blond kid who was sitting in a corner of the elevator, chewing gum rapidly and totally detached from the real world around him.

"You're thinking he's America's future, aren't you?" my beloved whispered.

"I'm tired of hearing comments like that."

"Thank God."

"But for me, he's still like an ear of corn whose seeds have landed in polluted water."

"You can never get that tired!"

"I can still see visions and hear prophecies."

My beloved chose to make light of my comment, not even bothering to respond with a mere hand gesture. I started looking at the black woman again, as beautiful as a winter morning in our village. I stare intently at her, fascinated, just as I used to do with little streams. Just then, her eyes glare at me like two gun muzzles. My discomfort is obvious enough, and I shudder. I wonder why I look away and withdraw into myself rather than giving her a smile and saying something pleasant. I feel nothing but admiration for her, so why am I being such a coward?

"How tall did she say the monument was?" I hear my beloved ask.

"As tall as Mikado!"

My beloved realizes I am referring to a tall, thin man in Kafrun who was named, or rather nicknamed, Mikado in the period when the notion of the Orient was flourishing.

I am glad the elevator has reached the top before my beloved has a chance to comment. I pull myself together and exit toward the windows from which we can observe the city of Washington spread-eagled naked in front of us, enticing and uninhibited: the Potomac River twists like a belly-dancer, splaying out like arteries, cuddling small, thickly forested islands that separate the city of Washington—the man—from the state of Virginia—the woman—who, with no apparent discrimination, announces that she is for lovers, evoking the little streams of Kafrun that we called rivers.

"Ah me, Tawfiq!" I say to myself.

I must have said his name out loud.

"Who's Tawfiq?" my beloved asks.

With a chuckle I remind her of an incident from long ago. As a child I used to run away from school and follow goat herders. One day I went with them to the Mall'ua Plain that overlooks Kafrun Valley. I sat down on a high rock close by Eagle's Nest and let my thoughts roam far and wide. I tracked the streams we called rivers to their sources, followed their waters as they seeped into the roots of trees and started to grow like a willow. Branches, green leaves, and wild blossoms sprouted from my skin. I turned into a sycamore, a grapevine, an oak, and a fig tree in a rock. All of a sudden, a sharp slap on my neck brought me back me to reality in a hurry. I turned round to find Tawfiq fuming with anger. "You ass, your goats have eaten the olive bushes!"

When Tawfiq realized he'd made a mistake, he apologized. The goats were not mine, nor was I in any way responsible for them. That evening he arrived at our house with grapes, figs, and green corncobs. Every time I go back to visit Kafrun, Tawfiq, I think of visiting you in Mall'ua. No doubt you're old now. How I wish I could meet your family.

Moving to another window we look out at the Lincoln Memorial. I see him, seated there for all time, silently contemplating a history that has slipped from his grasp and assumed forms he could never imagine. He looks wary, as though pressing his back against the wall for fear that Booth may fire at him again. He pays no attention to General Lee, who stares down at him from the top of a hill on the other shore of the river. He watches visitors as they climb the many steps; by the time they reach him they are exhausted. They read his words inattentively, as though such thoughts have no relevance to their present lives. I ask him whether he was deceiving himself or others when he spoke of government of the people, by the people, for the people. I challenge him to admit that actually there are governing and governed classes. He scoffs at the challenge, and I accuse him of being scared of the charge of Marxism.

With that he loses his temper with me and all those other annoying visitors. Disregarding his surroundings he withdraws inside himself and resorts to silence. I see him wondering why they constructed a reflecting pool for him. Were they trying to suggest that he should constantly contemplate himself and reconsider his career? His words are there, etched in stone, and cannot be reformulated. Why did they build the State Department so close to him? Perhaps it would have been even worse if they had erected his memorial next to the White House, for then he would be forced to witness his successors sleeping in his bed, repeating his words out of context and devoid of their real significance. You said: There is no escape from history; it determines the path we follow. I tell you, your successors have followed a path very different from the one to which you aspired.

We move to another window: And you, Jefferson, I accuse you of insisting on ideals that no longer play any role in history. Had you used your strategic position to observe Congress closely, you would have realized that fact with disarming rapidity. Forgive me for asking you a provocative question: Did you own slaves at the same time as you were talking about equality as a natural right? I wonder, did you understand this essential contradiction and decide to ignore it, or was your conception of man not generous and inclusive enough to include blacks, Native Americans, and others who fell outside your circle? Are people equal? All people? What was your tacit position on slavery? Do governments derive their powers from the will of the governed? Which of the governed? Are the people entitled to abolish governments? Are they entitled to abolish systems? And at the present time, are societies of the Third World entitled to shape their own future? What is your opinion of American society today? Are you a bridge between Europe and America and between the eighteenth and nineteenth centuries? Do you have any significance in modern times?

Forgive me, I realize these questions are taboo, but they pursue me relentlessly like my own shadow. I am obsessed by them. I am not trying to embarrass you or to expose your inconsistencies. Perhaps you are more tolerant than those who bear your heritage. Just look how Congress sits cross-legged atop the Mall like an old Turkish sultan bloated with time; within its purview sit the National Museums, just like maidens displaying their natural and acquired jewels. Beneath the dome—that lofty turban—nest swarms of wild hornets, buzzing incessantly and confusing their buzzing noises with real debate. Do you see, as I do, that this buzzing—the debate—is really a lottery for resources of the Third World, a world that finds itself perpetually crucified but never given a burial in case it should awaken and shake the foundation of the system? I doubt that will ever happen. And, once again without trying to embarrass you, I wonder if you share my opinion of the George Washington monument as an erect penis pointing up into the sky?

From another window we look down on 16th Street, which, beginning from the White House, separates the whites from the blacks. I see these two worlds as permanently separate, coming together only in political speeches. How can the hungry meet the overfed? How does master meet slave? Or weak meet strong? Or ruler ruled? Or poverty culture and wealth culture?

On the horizon sprawls the Pentagon, lazy and flaccid, surrounded by enormous parking lots filled with colorful cars. Ah, Norman Morrison, which Americans remember your name now? Were you crazy enough to immolate yourself in front of this cathedral of war, right under the window of the Secretary of Defense, to protest against America's war in Vietnam? The flames from your body rose twelve feet in the air, just like the voices of the wretched rising. Why did you decide to immolate your daughter with you? Was that your way of celebrating her first birthday? To whom did you want to offer her as a sacrifice?

The gods died long, long ago. These days, is there anyone alive who deserves sacrifices? When you changed your mind and threw your daughter out of the fire, you gave her back her own life, all so that you might burn to death alone. That was a good deed you did! Hundreds of poems were written for her. Do flames and poetry go together? After your spectacular immolation the war went on for years. For how many seconds did you feel the burning? In that single moment of your short life what agonies did you go through? So today's followers of the one crucified on the cross consider it madness that someone should sacrifice himself for a great cause. Your name fills the Vietnam sky; there they celebrate you as a hero and a martyr. Does it make any sense that America does not even recognize your name? Whether it does or not, your death was not in vain. You will endure outside and in spite of the country's consciousness. What a bitterly cruel irony that martyrdom should still be a necessity. How long must that remain so? To whom must we offer ourselves in sacrifice? Why? When? Does anyone deserve our eternal immolation? I agree, Richard Wagner, that these days (and perhaps in other ages too) the gods and their representatives on earth are sinners. It is mankind's task to save them.

While I am still preoccupied with my own questions, my beloved is involved in a lengthy conversation with a nervous tourist. The woman wants to talk about herself. She says she was born and raised in Knoxville, Tennessee. She loved the Smoky Mountains, but had to move to New York. For a long time she lived there alone with her dog, amid the throngs of people. Then a killer began roaming the city streets, seeking his victims among beautiful women, so she decided to travel to Europe. However she did not stay away for long, for a killer of a different type appeared. Home once again she felt more relaxed, but could not remember the name of a single person whom she could contact and share her feelings with. Then she was raped. Her neighbors heard her screaming, but no one bothered to help her or call the police. With that, she headed south again and returned to the Smoky Mountains' streams, before they too were invaded by tourists from the north.

# The Atmosphere of Sadness

Were my beloved to speak, she would tell this tourist about the routine life we lead. But she would be able to assure the woman that, in spite of a life of perpetual travel, she never feels lonely. As a child my beloved and her family moved from Aitha al-Fukhar village in the Beqaa Valley to Beirut, where they lived in an apartment facing Mount Sanin. The family was a large one, and they had many close friends. At the core of the family's relationships and struggles stood her mother, a capable and ambitious woman who had high aspirations for her children's future. She did not allow her husband to continue working as a taxi driver, especially after he had an accident that left a permanent scar on his forehead. Instead she urged him to emigrate to America. He joined his brothers and their families in Toledo, Ohio, and lived there for seven years, working as a painter and a guard. He became a U.S. citizen and sent for his family to join him. While in Ohio, he longed for the days of old when he used to drive his car proudly between Aitha, Zahla, Damascus, and Beirut. On weekends he would take his family to Wadi al-Arayish, the Kharizat Spring, Baalbek, Hama, Bludan, and Saidnaya. In his own country he felt he was in charge, whereas in America he felt like an ant dragging a large (and maybe empty) kernel of wheat, all the while scared of being trampled underfoot. Even so he was well aware that every river in the world empties into the American Ocean. He took heart at that and thanked God for this new grace.

The family settled in Detroit where my beloved's businessmen uncles lived. One of them was very rich, but a skinflint with himself and others as well. The second brother was middle-aged, single, religious, and financially secure. The youngest had died when his family had refused to let him be hospitalized because of their rigid religious convictions. The family struggled hard to rise above poverty level. My beloved did not finish her schooling, but left early to work in a woman's clothing store. Later on, she got a job as an accountant in a health insurance company. Her elder brother completed his studies and graduated with an engineering degree. The youngest brother, meanwhile, liked to work, but he liked women even more. My beloved came home from America, and we got married. Her elder brother came home too and married a beautiful girl who had moved with her family from the village of Deir Meemas in southern Lebanon. The youngest brother complicated his family's life by falling in love with a Catholic American girl who insisted—or rather, her family did—that he convert and marry her in their church. When he refused, the family moved the girl far away to the north. Deep within her, she still nurses a wound he may never see.

In light of these events, the family held a meeting. It was decided that Mansur should return to the old country with his mother and look for a bride. The mother said as much at the meeting, but the boy's father protested that their financial situation ruled out the idea. My beloved suggested that the boy go alone and find a wife for himself. The elder brother thought Mansur should graduate and find work first before getting married.

Mansur returned to the old country with his mother and started looking for a wife. He missed his American girlfriend and kept looking for a woman who looked like her. His mother on the other hand wanted someone tall, pretty, and white (because Mansur was short and dark), someone from a notable family who was also a university graduate (so she could work while Mansur completed his studies). Relatives and friends came up with a number of suggestions. There were many invitations and daily visits involving endless rounds of coffee. Sometimes dinner or lunch was heavy; the burning sensation Mansur got was more often in his stomach than in his heart. After many failed attempts, they returned to America without a wife. He felt terribly lonely and thought of his ex-girlfriend in the north. At such times, he regretted not marrying Suad. He remembered the trip they took together in the grey car from the sea and cedars to Sidon, Zahla, and Baalbek. In the green mountains he had felt he was being carried on the wings of an eagle circling high above valleys that were as deep as his own wounded heart. In the Beqaa Valley he could smell traces of incense as they wafted upwards from ancient temples. By the seashore he worked on his suntan while filling his chest with wind and spray. He remembered their discussion about America, while her family was busy studying his mother much more closely than they were him. That gave him a certain latitude to develop his relationship with Suad. He had told her unequivocally that he was not the type to marry without love or to expect his bride to be some kind of undiscovered virgin island rich in rain, trees, and sun that no man had ever discovered before him or would in the future. When he told her that, she had blushed—he was not sure why. Perhaps she thought he was trying to trick her into a confession.

At the time he regretted not getting married, but felt he had made the right decision by not rushing into a marriage just because he had traveled home for that purpose. He realized that he had placed himself in an awkward situation, searching for a bride as though looking for an apartment to rent. This was not what he wanted for himself. He wanted his marriage to be spontaneous. He wanted to be in love first, not to fall into an arranged marriage. In spite of all these realizations, he agreed to let his mother ask for Suad's hand from her family. Her family agreed on condition that they elope so as to avoid the wedding expenses. He thought of his mother and her grandmother in the vineyard, meeting to negotiate the details of the elopement, and had a good laugh. However, when negotiations became difficult, he realized how risky his actions were and made a firm decision to withdraw.

When he returned to the United States, he met and fell in love with another American girl. He married her even though his family was unhappy about it, but it didn't take long for them to accept the marriage. The family's financial situation improved, and they were careful to avoid any behavior that might destroy the many achievements they had accomplished in such a short space of time. The family became wealthy, and owned several houses and cars. They had struggled long and hard, but at the very moment of their success they suddenly found themselves paying a high price.

The eldest brother took his father, his aunt, his wife, and his little girl on a trip to Boston. On their way, they visited the Niagara Falls and took pictures of the mighty waterfall pouring awesomely into the heart of the world. The next day they continued on to Boston. They never arrived. On the New York Thruway their car's tire exploded, and they spun off the road at a fatal speed, slamming into a bridge. The brother, his wife, and the aunt were killed instantly. The father died on the way to the hospital and the little girl was permanently handicapped. The girl's grandmother cared for her for years before committing her to an institution where she lives to this day. The doctor explained to them that the accident had turned the child's brain into something like a broken egg, its yolk mixed with its white.

The cruelest part of this tragedy was the way the police conveyed the news to my wife's mother. They went to her home in Detroit, where she was alone with her grandson who at the age of fifteen months had just become an orphan. Tersely and with no finesse they simply told her what had happened. They made a routine inquiry as to whether there was anything she needed, then left. She telephoned us in Ann Arbor. Without tears she told us about the accident, but went on to say that everyone was in the hospital. We drove to the family home at breakneck speed, our minds preoccupied with the specter of death. Once we go there, it was indeed death that we had to face, sharp as a sword blade.

We had to make a fresh start. Yet in such circumstances who on earth can simply put grief behind him and venture forth as though liberated from the concerns of the past? The mother certainly could not. She remained at home, her heart, eyes, forehead, and clothes all enveloped in a dark cloud. Nor could Mansur forget. Suddenly he found himself isolated and alone, forced to take on an ever-growing pile of responsibilities that confronted him at home, at turns in the road, and at night once his bride had fallen asleep. She had no idea how to cope with the new situation. All she wanted was for her husband to forget and go back to their previous way of life, as though nothing had happened. Death, she told him, was the end for the dead, but not for those still living. She wanted him to keep going out with her to bars, theaters, and restaurants, but he could not. How could he? He tried it once, but burst into tears inside a crowded restaurant and rushed out. She had to leave her dinner and chase after him. As year followed year, things went from bad to worse. They had four children, but eventually she declared their relationship a failure and left him to go in search of a new life, something she never found. Mansur still bears his enormous responsibilities, as heavy as his own ancient past.

Death served to unite me with my beloved, our oneness born of happiness and deepened by sadness. We experienced it together. We became absorbed in the present and journeyed fearlessly into the labyrinth of past and future. We sallied forth in different directions, surveying the world from below and above; from the middle of the crowd, from inside the belly of a whale; from the seas and the lofty skies.

So this is how things began and how we expect them to end. My beloved had returned to Beirut; we only met again after a six-year separation. In the interim we wrote to each other; our letters were mostly about unimportant things. Only in the vaguest of terms did we allude to the most important topic of all, in the process veiling our words in a dense cloud-cover, just like the one we flew through over the ocean.

Once, when I was a boy, my friend Faris invited me to spend a week in Aitha al-Fukhar as a way of getting away from Beirut's oppressive heat. I did not hesitate. Like birds released from their cage we took off, flying high above the mountains and hovering over the Beqaa Valley. Skirting the main road leading to the ancient gate of Damascus, a gate as ancient as humanity, we followed a narrow winding path along the western foothills of the eastern mountains. We picked grapes in a lentil field called Bayadir al-Adas and entered a valley surrounded on three sides by bare hills. Aitha al-Fukhar is not like Kafrun, but it has a beauty of its own. (I say this for my beloved to hear). Its unique beauty comes from its cool dry air, clear sky, and long walks in the vineyards. Since I was from Kafrun, I asked about springs. Faris said there was a freshwater spring where girls often gathered, so at sunset we walked there. There we found incredible bevies of girls, all waiting in line to fill their jars with water. We loitered around them. So who was to be the bee and who the flower? Who would start the game of seduction? How and why?

Boundaries are blurred, but why ask questions when the game is driven by such intensity? O, the doves of a thousand and one nights! How were cloistered girls transformed into doves flying nonstop to a clear lake? How did the same doves then change back into beautiful girls swimming naked, oblivious of the world around them? Are you so sexually deprived, Qamar al-Zaman, that you have to watch them from behind a rock, an outcrop, or a tree; and then decide to steal one of the girls' dresses and her magic hat, the one that turns her into a dove and enables her to escape her confines and fly away to freedom? Why did you imprison her in your mother's palace and leave her in a dark room with no windows? I know that she will search for a lover in the dark corridors; then maybe you'll grab her and even cast stones at her. Your life will be no richer for it, you petty tyrant.

Then there appeared the girl who has become my beloved, my life companion, and my partner in this adventure of joy and sadness. She was like a cluster of grapes hanging from a tall tree over Shaykh Hasan's spring. I had no desire to pick the grapes; it was an even greater delight just to contemplate them. No imprisonment, no theft, no rooms without windows. The space is the house of dreams. She fills the jar with water; with it I am filled.

I turned to Faris. "Is there such beauty in Aitha?" I asked.

"Do you like her?"

"She takes my breath away."

"Shall we spend the evening at her house? Her brothers are friends of mine."

"Your friends are my friends."

That night the world expanded; walls and boundaries fell away. We spent the evening sitting on the roof at her house, a group of young men and women. I recalled the seasons when wheat is cooked, bulghur is crushed, kishik is prepared, swings are strung, and love songs are sung in Kafrun. In the moonlight we walked to the vineyards and the harvest fields. The girl who was to become my beloved sang a love song, I recited some love poetry, and we all danced the dabka to Faris's drum and to Layla's singing.

I met the girl who was to become my beloved many times in Aitha and later in Beirut. We argued about politics and religion; she called me a radical, and I retorted by telling her that her political awareness was a sham. Later on, I was amazed (and she must have been too) at the boldness (or maybe the sheer impudence) with which I spoke to her on that occasion. What authority allowed me to talk to her in such terms? Was I already in love with her? However, what really matters is that our relationship was strengthened without any need for reassurance or confirmation. Once, during an intimate conversation with her (and I can't remember what it was that took us in this particular direction), I heard myself saying, "If the world turned into a river . . . ."

I wasn't expecting a positive response, so I was taken aback when she added: "And we were turned into fish . . . ."

"We'd live inside the currents . . . ."

"And glide freely in different directions . . . ."

"Do fish flirt with each other?"

"By the way, I can't swim. Will you teach me?"

"I am not one to pass up wonderful opportunities."

However, before that opportunity presented itself, before we had developed our own symbolic language, and even before we had determined whether fish flirt, my beloved emigrated to the United States with her family. We exchanged a few letters without revealing our love (except a few hints here and there) and without making any commitments. But, when she came back years later, I was both overjoyed and bewildered. We spent New Year's Eve at Cafe Nasr in al-Rawsha with my friend Asaad and another woman with whom I had set him up. To this day he asks me why I was so keen to exact such a severe penalty. A fight broke out among some drunks, and the police showed up. Many customers seized the opportunity to leave without paying, but we did not. I had to revisit my conviction that I'm not one to miss opportunities, especially since I'm not an admirer of businessmen. I could easily have come up with convincing excuses, but I may have been anxious to leave her with a positive impression.

With my beloved's return after many years the world had indeed turned into a river and we into colorful fish. We swam freely in different directions and depths, but then we were caught in a net and snatched from the water. We struggled for a little while before being tossed into the marriage pool; in fact we may well have entered the net of our own accord. We still see the world as a river and swim freely in different directions, albeit still within the marriage pool.

We emigrated to the United States and lived in Ann Arbor, where I continued my studies at the University of Michigan. We took part in the black civil rights movement and in demonstrations against the American involvement in Vietnam. I will never forget the long line of American students in front of the library waiting to donate blood to Vietnamese revolutionaries by way of Algeria. And I will never forget that a number of my colleagues were involved in establishing a student movement for a democratic society. Where are you now, Tom Hayden? You married Jane Fonda, the movie star, and struggled to become a political star yourself. Martin Luther King's assassination pierced the heart of the nonviolence movement like a bullet, burying it forever. From its grave emerged the doctrine of Black Power. But then it was that doctrine's turn to be assassinated as well. What can we do when both nonviolence and violence fail? Surrender? Impossible. Does the Rainbow Coalition provide a solution? Whatever the case, the struggle will continue.

The day I returned to my homeland, I wrote the following: "How wonderful it is to come home! How wonderful when hands are held, shoulders touch, and voices rise in song."

*We shall overcome*
*We shall overcome some day*
*Deep in my heart I do believe*
*We shall overcome some day.*

The day Martin Luther King, who had long since overcome all fear of death, was assassinated, I wrote, "Those who have transcended violence (Socrates, Jesus, Gandhi, and King) were all killed by violence. But from his wounds another leader will emerge, and he will challenge us, saying, 'To hell with my life, I know I will die.'" In America, I used to find myself singing ataba on my way to exams, sometimes out loud, and these verses in particular:

*From afar are heard echoes of caravan bells,*
*Reminding me of days gone by,*
*To the city I brought my wares to sell,*
*A stranger from whom no one cared to buy.*

Like others, I relived my own culture by eating kibbeh, tabouleh, hummus, and ful and by dancing the dabka. As the seasons changed, we would often stroll along the banks of the River Huron. In wintertime when it was frozen, we picked the flowers; in spring we gathered grape leaves; in summer we plunged into its cooling water; and in fall we watched as the birds migrated south. With Rashid we fished in the silver lake and in another lake we nicknamed "old man" lake because an old man inhabited its shores.

During crises we made fruitless attempts to explain the Palestinian cause to other people. How many doors in democratic households were firmly closed! Is it out of sheer ignorance that we knock on doors even when we don't expect an answer? Why bother? Are mines more effective? We tried using the dabka as a way of introducing our popular traditions to the people of Michigan's thumb area, but that was just as useless. We were dispersed throughout the world's labyrinths. Khalid and Shafiqa, stable times in Beirut are long gone. Instead our lives are suspended in a nebula of fog, fire, and ice. Muhammad, his mother's only son, has stayed on in Beirut, but divorced twice and married a third wife. His future is still before him, if he can stay alive.

# The Messiah Dances in the Moonlight and Swims Naked

Faced with the perennial question of where to settle, we decided to try Boston for a while. We followed exactly the same life rituals as in Beirut, and as we do in Washington now: we get up in the morning, drink our coffee while reading the newspaper (in Beirut we used to sit on our apartment balcony in Showeifat and observe its fertile desert); breakfast over, we leave for work or wander the city streets, without guidance or direction.

Once we went up the John Hancock Tower to observe Boston from above. We went up, maybe to the sixtieth floor, and looked out on the Charles River, Boston Harbor, Logan Airport, Beacon Hill, Harvard University, and in the distance the White Mountains in New Hampshire.

It was as though my beloved knew exactly what was going through my mind at that precise moment. She started mimicking me—proof positive that by now we had developed our own symbolic language. Looking down on the city from such a tremendous height was a wonderful experience. We had had enough of immersing ourselves in partials and details. It was really wonderful, indeed essential, to get the broader picture; to see the way things connect and discover the incredible way they coalesce, creating a yet greater whole that turns into a new entity even more amazing and important than the sum of its parts. In fact it isn't the individual elements that are unique, but rather the linkages between them. That applies, of course, to individuals as well as to society. Certainly the individual isn't just a thing; he or she is the very acme of consciousness. However, society is the acme of creation; it is only within its borders that perception, mind, soul, personality, and God are created. The truth is that God is a symbol of society beginning with the father. He is a symbol of the whole that transcends its parts.

My beloved stops mimicking me and my ideas. "When will you ever forget your sociological studies," she asks me in her own unique fashion, "stop analyzing things just for a moment, and remake yourself?"

"I'm an analytical person."

"But what about fun, life, and spontaneity, stupid?"

"Always, my sweet, always!"

"Hey, watch out! You just bumped into that lady!"

"She should watch out!"

I turn my attention away from this interruption by mimicking her imitations of me: As long as we cannot break free from space, let's try to liberate ourselves from the lowest level and mere details. Let's rise to the top, climbing as high as possible. From there we can survey the lower levels. We'll feel we're soaring. It's the way I felt when climbing Mount al-Sayida or the Eagle's Nest in Kafrun. Do you get the feeling that your heart is being snatched from your chest whenever you look down from a high spot? I feel wings growing and, to my surprise, I'm soaring. My heart is snatched away and bursts from its nest like a crane, rising and flapping its wings. It is a really wonderful experience for someone to be snatched away and to grow wings so he can roam the wide, wide skies.

My beloved puts her hand on my shoulder. "Let's go down," she says. "I'm afraid you'll fly away."

"I'll carry you on my wings."

"Cut it out. Come on, let's go down."

"What's the hurry? Do you remember when we visited Munir and Husni in Chicago?"

"The day you insisted on going up the Prudential building?"

"I seem to remember that you insisted we stay there for a long time."

"Right. It was nighttime. The streets looked like rivers of light. White rivers with orange ones running parallel."

"It's been a while since we've seen Husni and Safiyya."

"That's true."

Once more we descended to the city abyss. I held my beloved's hand, lacing my fingers in hers, as we roamed the streets and gardens. We turned toward Harvard Square, and from there to a nearby park. The music was noisy and the song defiant, a protest against hegemonic authority. The early seventies were a revolution in fashion and lifestyles, a revolution sponsored by the affluent; a luxurious protest against a system that guarantees them a luxurious life. With my fingers laced in my beloved's, I watched young girls baring their bodies. One of them lay on her back, sunning herself and listening attentively to the noisy music. She was exposing as much of her body as possible; scantily dressed in tight shorts, she had unfastened her bra, allowing her nipples to savor the fresh air. I took a picture of her, focusing the lens on the cave of emeralds and pearls. That same day I went on a sea voyage from island to island. Next I focused the camera lens on the breasts of a girl who was dancing by herself; her eyes were closed and she was completely lost to the world. When I seemed to be taking a more than appropriate interest in her, my beloved remarked, "She's obviously high!"

"She has beautiful breasts. That's what counts."

"So have your fill of the view!"

But I did not have my fill. On the contrary, I felt a heightened sensation of an ancient craving. I watched as one of her breasts slipped out of her shirt, which lay wide open like books of sacred scripture. It quivered like a colorful bird that just a moment ago had discovered the secret of flying, and then, scared and reckless in equal measure, was trying to fly in every direction. I put some rare seeds in my palm and opened it wide, hoping that it might perch on my fingers and take what it wanted. But I waited in vain. I soon turned my attention to a tall, thin youth who was impersonating the Messiah. He had long hair and beard and was carrying a staff just like the one I used to carry in Kafrun to pick pomegranates, figs, walnuts, and clusters of grapes that only the birds could reach. Was that why the Messiah carried a staff, I wondered?

Coming up with that question made me happy; it made me feel I'd suddenly discovered some eternal truth, despite my conviction that there are no such things. I wondered if our lives in Kafrun were very like the life that the Messiah led. Did he swim naked, roam fields, clamber up mountains, and hide behind oleander and sycamore branches, watching girls swimming?

In spite of cultural distances, the youth in Boston impersonating the Messiah addressed a group of people gathered around him. I ask you, who is the antithesis of the Messiah in this disdainful era? You would be surprised, and I can understand why. Plentiful are those who claim to be Christian in this society founded on violence. Violence is a daily activity, a kind of recreation. Leisure itself has turned violent. Love is violence; sports, writing, university, music, they're all violence. But I meant something more specific by my question—a certain role. The moneychangers whom Christ chased out of the temple, they're not the only antithesis to the Messiah. It is not just politicians who practice oppression, nor capitalists who starve the world in order to stuff themselves. The one who speaks in the Messiah's name is also his antithesis. Frankly, the Pope is the antithesis of the Messiah. To be sure, he is a crowned king; he's the king of kings. Look at the stately chariot they use to carry him inside on their shoulders. Look at the jewels, the scepter, the bodyguards, and the entourage. Don't be deceived by his humility—he is a ruler just like every other ruler. They have turned believers into a submissive herd. Now, compare all this with the life of the Messiah. He was barefoot and starving, with long, flowing hair and torn clothing. He didn't associate with politicians, priests, merchants, or the wealthy. He was a friend of the indigent, the sick, the tortured, and the poor. He discussed the details of their lives with them and would not allow them to prostrate themselves. Through Him they stood tall. They opened up to Him from the inside like a daisy. He encouraged them to make discoveries, to liberate themselves, and not to cling to blind faith or empty rituals. Traditions were made for man, not vice versa. Mankind invented traditions, so in this miserable era of ours why should he be turned into a tool? Mind, spirit, and body, they are all dominated by a false consciousness. Can we combine the establishment and revolution? Which one is the antithesis of which? I tell you, in this miserable era everything is the antithesis of everything else. Role and person are opposed, just as the establishment is the opposite of revolution. The establishment and the larger role it represents insist on blessing the poor, and yet it still refuses to let them have a class-consciousness. This is not the language of the Messiah! It's the jargon of businessmen, capitalists, and rulers. I tell you all very frankly that Christianity has changed. No longer is it a faith for the abandoned, the weak, the poor, the sick, and the impoverished. It has turned into a religion for the elite, the powerful, the wealthy, and the overfed. It is an establishment, one that is linked to the other establishments and the overall system.

There were other equally interesting scenes, so I turned the camera lens away from the Messiah of this age to a young man wearing lipstick, earrings, a necklace and women's shoes; to a girl whose boyfriend had stolen her bra, so she chased after him without even bothering to cover up her swaying breasts; to a group of Hare Krishnas shaking their tambourines, singing, dancing, and collecting donations; then to a dog that was totally absorbed in the noisy scene, running all over the place and circling a George Washington statue in order to urinate on a spot where someone had scratched out the original inscription and written instead in a pale scrawl, "Democracy is Rape."

Now here we are, my beloved and I, fifteen years later, fingers intertwined, wandering around Washington rather than Boston. Things have changed a lot. Self-indulgence remains a primary value. Success is once again crowned king, erecting a monument to competition on the ruins of friendship. Clothing fashions have changed. Today's youth are elegant; they like to read glossy media magazines, very nationalistic and angry at the third world. "Who are these backward peoples," they ask, "who dare to challenge the greatest power in history?" Yes, fashions have changed, but a preoccupation with them has not. The essential element is one and the same: counterculture and dominant culture both represent self-indulgence in an affluent society.

I don't believe my beloved was thinking about the same things. Unlike my expression, hers reflected inner tranquility, like a white cloud floating over an inlet that goes deep inland. Perhaps she was thinking again about our situation. We had ventured into the wide world to forget, but is that possible? How can my mother forget the present and still remember the remote past? She can still recall the people who were closest to her in childhood; she mentions their names and has a real conversation with them. So where, I ask myself, are the borders between reality and illusion? How does illusion turn into reality and vice versa? What's the point of living in this nebulous world? And isn't it weird to return from illusion to reality and speak with such utter clarity? Many times my mother has called me "Uncle Rashid, Uncle Rashid." I have told her that I'm her son, not her uncle, to which she has replied by way of clarification, "You're my uncle, my father, my mother, my brother, my sister, my son, and everything that's dear to me."

I was astonished and took refuge in silence. She was silent for a moment too, but then she went on to herself, "You left me, Isbir. You're lucky to have died. I'm the one whose soul God refuses to take. Give me some poison so I can die. Take care of the girl. Feed her."

I ask her who the girl is, but she doesn't answer. I'm trying to understand. She talks about many things. Then all of a sudden I realize she means herself. She has become her own daughter, the girl she lost in early childhood.

When we brought her back home, she changed. In the hospital she had no idea where she was, nor does she now. Even so, she should have noticed some kind of change in her surroundings. I asked her to sing, and she did not hesitate. In a faint, cracking voice, she tried to sing a verse of ataba:

*Three, four, and two are nine*
*Your heart throbs as mine*
*Where are the knights of chivalry*
*To unlock the iron chains around my neck?*

Many times I had heard her singing, but never before had I heard this particular verse of ataba. What mattered was that Halim's mother was a fighter. At that particular moment I got the impression that she was going to triumph over death once again. My feelings were further confirmed when she moved from the ataba song to a fine rhythmic tune like the ones that the best vocalists sing at parties:

*Look at the beauty standing by the well!*
*Her cheeks are as soft as silk.*
*I loved you when you were young*
*Long before your breasts had fully blossomed.*
*Pour down, you tears, pour forth!*

I couldn't believe what I was hearing. Halim's mother knew such songs and could still repeat them? Impossible! What sort of world was stirring in her memory so threatened with disintegration? What repressed moments were these? An atmosphere of grief returns, as she intones another ataba verse, one I could hardly understand, except for this little strophe:

*Where have my beloved ones gone?*
*Like a bird with clipped wings am I!*

I asked her to repeat it. She tried but couldn't. "I'm tired," she said and fell asleep.

"Is this reawakening possible?" I asked myself. "Is her sleep full of nightmares or dreams? In her life is sleep any different from being awake?"

I asked her this same question over and over again. On one occasion I told her that her jumbled words sounded like nonsense. "I say what I see in my sleep," was her response. I couldn't believe what I had heard and only wished that Freud could have heard what she said.

She was sound asleep, and I was completely awake. I found myself answering a question that I had never been able to answer before: when did I learn to write and who influenced me? I must have been influenced by you, mother, without even realizing it. You must be a poet yourself if, even from within your own hazy world, you can still manage to say, "We can never get enough of the people we love." You are a poet, a fighter. You feel sad but, as you often repeat, not unlucky. "Please, relieve me of this tiring life," you plead, and you go on to ask God, "O Lord, why are you targeting me?" God doesn't answer, so you sing to yourself:

*Tears of worry flow down my cheeks*
*None can dispel my heart's distress.*
*Methought tranquility overcomes anxiety,*
*But 'tis anxiety that wins the day.*

Must this be what you are feeling now? If things were different, would you change the verse? Would it still be poetry? Is poetry a verse or a vast expanse?

I have long thought of my father as a crane. Are you a crane too, mother? And you, O crane, how do you see yourself? What language do you speak to yourself, to the trees, the clouds, the rain, and the water? Is your language akin to the language of water? When you soar over land, what is your relationship to the wind? What do you observe, what do you search for? Do you consider the sky your tent? Do you read the alphabet of the stars? Will you accept my father and mother among your flocks? In the future will you accept me too? Will you live long? What will you do when you can no longer fly? Will you experience a lingering death? I tell you, my mother is dying a slow death. Medicine cannot cure her, but it will not let her die with dignity either. "Please relieve me of this tiring life," she yells at me from the depths of despair. How can I relieve her? Could it be that what is really bothering me is relieving myself of the exhaustion involved in dealing with her? I doubt it. Today, this very day, I heard her singing alone and to herself:

*O sad woman, you are not worn out.*
*The steel bridge may have eroded, but not you.*

I apologize, O crane, for burdening you with my problems, but I need to tell you something else, just one more thing before I change the subject. Yesterday my brother remarked that my mother's body seemed stronger but her mind was weaker. "That means," he went on, "she's going to need more and more care." "And for a long time," I replied with a sigh of regret.

Forgive me, I'll change the subject. Let me tell you: one of our neighbors in a Washington suburb had a sticker on her car that said, "If you're rich, I'm single." I thought that provided enough of a cue for talking to her, so I said, "I'm poor, so you're married." Nothing I've said seems to amuse you. Listen to something else: Let me tell you about my mother—sorry to return to the same subject. Whenever she was in a fix, she used to repeat a line of prayer. These days, she's suffering from constipation. So when she goes to the bathroom, she prays in a high voice, "Through the mediation of the mother of God, O savior, save us."

O crane, you seem not to be able to laugh! Why? Has your life lacked tranquility? We all need some once in a while. A short time ago, I crossed over to her shore. "God bless you, O smart mother of Halim," I said to her at one point. "You can bury such smartness," was her reply.

I wish you'd smile just a little, O crane. Yesterday I went into my mother's room and found her frowning. "What's the matter?" I asked. "Your expression looks like Abu Ali's backside." Do you know what her answer was? "Why," she said, "have you ever seen it?"

# The Joys and Pains of the Pigeons

We must have had our fill of watching the city's nakedness. Throwing a parting glance at the Potomac, we went down to continue our walk along the Mall. We sat down next to an old man feeding pigeons. One of them approached him confidently and pecked pieces of bread from his hand.

"Why do we Arabs call boys' private parts 'pigeons'?" I asked my beloved.

"Weird!"

"Really, I want to know."

"You are back to your hallucinations!"

"I know a beautiful woman named 'joys of the pigeon.'"

My beloved had a good laugh at that. An American woman stopped right by us. "Speak English," she said angrily, "you're in America."

We were astonished. I gave her a derisory glance. My beloved gestured to me to ignore her. "You don't need to dignify her with a reply," she said.

We continued our walk, but I could not help thinking that I should have said something to annoy the woman, something like "I thought that there was freedom in America," or "We speak poetry, whereas English is just the language of commerce." I realized that she was an older woman, but I still didn't really understand. I found myself wanting to confront her, but she had disappeared in the crowd. It occurred to me that in their own countries Arabs are proud to speak foreign languages. Why? I remember your remark, Mahmud: Arabs find foreigners engaging when they make an effort to speak Arabic, even if they make mistakes, yet we judge ourselves harshly and make sarcastic remarks whenever one of us makes a small mistake in English or French. You are absolutely right, Mahmud. I wonder why it happens.

I turned to my beloved. "I've an idea," I said. "Why don't we go to the Shenandoah Mountains tonight and spend the night there?"

"That's a great idea, but I have to work tomorrow."

"Who cares?"

"Do you want to scale mountain peaks and be snatched away?"

"And go down to the waterfalls too if you like."

Without a moment's pause we made our way back to the car. Once we had descended the Washington Monument, the horizon had narrowed and the shape of the world changed. That's how we felt. The comment that woman had made was an announcement of our descent. We kept plunging through the crowd, cutting through the chaos as it cut through us, like tiny atoms colliding in a confined space.

We found ourselves on the road to Potomac Falls. Without even realizing it, we had taken a wrong turn on the way to Shenandoah. We carried on anyway. I remembered that there had been a thunderstorm the day before; the river would be high and the falls would be cascading furiously. In a strange way the roar of the falls reminded me of Beethoven's music; it had been some time since I had listened to the ninth symphony.

We arrived at a high bluff overlooking the river. As we expected, it was very turbulent. We walked toward the edge of the bluff. My hand sought my beloved's, and our fingers intertwined.

"Are you scared?" she asked.

"I think so."

"Your color's changed, and you're trembling."

"I enjoy and fear heights at the same time."

"I thought you liked flying."

"I do."

Instead of moving back, I found myself inching toward the edge and looking down at the river. The water was roaring headlong like a thousand tigers—foaming angrily, threatening and roiled up all at the same time. Plunging water makes an awesome sound, and the air was filled with a fine spray.

Something inside me breaks away. With every sinew in my body I feel it taking flight, just like a crane, wings flapping in the face of a vast sky, bursting through thick white clouds over the Atlantic and looking down on them from above. To the crane the clouds sometimes look like sheep grazing on Mall'ua Plain, at others like a cotton blanket enveloping the earth. It traverses the dense black rain clouds over Europe, soaring above Alpine peaks and following in the steps of Hannibal. It is enraptured by the Mediterranean sun and journeys with Sindbad from island to island. It searches for wayward Ulysses, eager to direct his steps back to the woman who awaits his return, and recalls the death of Socrates. When rain starts to fall over the sea, it approaches the Syrian shore, humble and apprehensive. It questions history as old as humanity's own wounds. Giving hunters a wide berth, it slows down over sad Antioch in search of ruins of libraries and temples, then hovers over the heights of Kasab, Slinfa, Qadmus, Misyaf and Jabal al-Qusair. Long and hard it contemplates "Hell's Valley," finding it strange that anything so beautiful could have such a name. It turns to glance at al-Hisn castle and

Safita's tower and gasps as it looks down from Bab al-Naqab on Kafrun Valley. Safely it lands, panting.

Now here I am, sitting on a fig-tree branch at al-Dahr overlooking Farah's garden, which he has named "Morning Star." I'm reclaiming my childhood, liberated from the aggravations of the present. Barefoot I wander through alleys, woods, orchards, springs, creeks, and rivers. I clamber up rocks, trees, hills, and mountains. I pick fruit the moment it is ripe, and stalk birds to their nests so I can bend over and look at their speckled eggs. Once I helped a bird kill a snake that was heading for its nest to eat the eggs. I established a competitive but friendly relationship with my own shadow, watching it stand tall and thin in the morning and then gradually shrink close to noon. Then we used to head back together and take a nap with the goats at the Makhada riverside. When my shadow started getting longer again, we would go back up the mountain; eventually, around sunset-time, it would once more stand tall and thin. Through my relationship with my shadow, I found myself transformed into a midget in the morning and evening and into a giant at noon. At night I thrust it out of my life. Whenever I wanted it to chase me, I would run toward the sun; when I preferred to chase it, the direction would be reversed. We chased each other, but there was no separation. Sometimes I might swerve to left or right, pivot round, or go forward or backward, all with the aim of throwing it off, but it was always on the alert, fully cognizant of all the secret ruses of the game. I was just as alert and aware, so I can't remember it ever beating me, but I don't recall ever beating it either. What matters is that my relationship with my shadow was always full of joy, regardless of the outcome.

Instead of getting readymade and expensive toys at religious festivals and acting all surprised, we used to make up our own games. One of the games Raif and I made up was to see who could pee the furthest. We figured out ways to pilfer walnuts, grapes, and pomegranates, and diverted water from irrigation ditches without getting caught by the watchman, whom we called "shubassi." Oh, Uncle Mighal! When they hired you to be the shubassi, you used to keep a watchful eye on us from the bay leaf canopy on your roof. I'll never forget the day we stole Ghali's pomegranates (and I'm not talking symbolically here). You waited for us in the alley at the back of Daas's house; that's where we found ourselves staring you in the eye with no hope of running away. You ordered us to spread our legs until we almost split, then beat us with a pomegranate branch. Even today I can still feel the sting of that pomegranate branch on my legs. I still can't understand how we were so compliant when our teachers, Jamil and Abdalla, told us to go into the garden and cut the pomegranate branches that they used to punish us. We always chose the best branches. How was it we become part of our own punishment? By the way, Uncle Mighal, who gave you that name? When did your father emigrate to Cuba? When did the emigrations start? Ah, emigration! Why were you so cruel? Being a friend of your son, Latif, was no help. I can still remember clearly when your son, Rifaat, died in early childhood. Would he have been as thin as you and as hard as the granite at al-Sheer Spring? The day you beat us, I didn't dare ask you, "Why don't you discipline your daughter, Latifa, the way you do us? She's meeting Hana al-Nadra in secret." But I liked Hana and Latifa and did not want you to know. In any case, it was completely futile to defy you. People would inform you about your children's offenses, but your response was always the same: "Honor just doesn't suit our family," you'd say sarcastically. They'd laugh at such amorous intrigues. Latifa and Hana, your children were very cute, and I still think of them a lot. I can understand what took them to Beirut, but it's a mystery to me what took them to Australia. Latif now lives in Germany, and Salwa in El Paso, Texas. Why are families so scattered?

And you! I'm not going to mention your name or even hint at it. That way, people in the village won't be able to guess. Why were you so cruel too? Now you're dead and buried deep under the soil, transformed into decayed bones. I will tell you now: I plucked your daughter's twin apricots before they turned into pomegranates, but, I assure you, I never ate them once she grew up. May God protect her honor as well as yours and mine. I'm only telling you this secret now so it'll rattle your bones in the grave, all that for being so unkind to us. What's wrong with liking apricots? I love them when they're beginning to bud. Unripe grapes dipped in salt are so delicious! I apologize to you. Isn't it mean to talk to you in the language of revenge? In fact, for that very reason I won't reveal this secret. Maybe you won't understand if I tell you that, for me, writing is a way of confessing long-repressed secrets.

Now it's your turn, Fuad. Why were you such a wild child? On my way to Bayt Badra two things used to scare me: one was you, the other was Shaykh Ali's dogs. I once heard a story (but I'm not sure it's true) that you used to climb the Sayida mountain and cast stones at God. I don't know if you really did that or if it was Mighal or Mikado. I suspect it was you. When you changed from a wild child into a gentle poet, your words would sometimes still explode in anger. "Oh my revolution," you said once, "away with a god such as this." You have a great deal of pride, I realize. As you get older and approach death, you still refuse to ask for forgiveness. Maybe you suppose that, because you write poetry, you're never going to die. I can tell you that I recently ran into Mikado and asked him if he still walks as fast as we remember. His reply was, "I still walk, run, and fly." I reminded him of the day he was carrying two baskets, one stuffed with imported goods from Tripoli and the other with eggs. I bought a pen from him in exchange for an egg. At that, he gave a hearty laugh and demanded more eggs, since that very pen had taught me the secret of writing.

Dear Fuad, we remembered you a lot recently when Abu Safa visited us in Washington. I was amazed how similar our memories were in spite of our age difference. Abu Safa wasn't surprised. He said we had similar recollections because we lived in the same environment: the same clear water, the same habitat, the same air, and the same birds; pomegranates, willows, sycamores, and oak trees; roads, alleys, and rocks—all the same. And people were the same too, generation after generation. His generation had preceded ours and was more deprived, but they managed to find delight in simple things that we enjoyed too. He spoke to me as though the past were a book in his palm: how he would go to the Makhada riverside, fall asleep under Shaykh Abdalla's oak trees, steal Umm Tansi's figs, hunt birds under the qurtuma tree, play marbles, checkers, and hopscotch, and drink water from the Frishlu spring. He also mentioned the barbecued meat at festivals, watermelon, fencing, fishing, and archery from atop defiant horses, fishing with bows and arrows, and stealing corn, walnuts, and pomegranates. Then, all of a sudden, he started reviewing the past from the perspective of the present. Everything he'd mentioned, he suggested, might sound trivial, particularly to people who had never experienced them. For us on the other hand, those very same things could (and still can) fire our imagination to break out of its normal confines and arouse thousands of feelings buried deep inside us. "Believe me," he added without the slightest exaggeration, "the good health I enjoy at age seventy-one is undoubtedly due to those good old days. It's all to do with clean air and bulghur cooked with green beans."

Abu Safa gave a hearty laugh, but then he went quiet, his expression transformed by dark clouds. I realize now that deep inside him some painful memories must have been stirred. As I expected, he went on to point out that our generation had it easier than his. As a child he had heard stories of people dying of hunger, with only Khalil Abbud to bury them. He used to carry them on his back and toss them into a deep pit. Skeletons used to pile up like pieces of dried firewood. He also recalled stories of men being taken away by the Turks to serve in the Turkish army; some of them came home to find their green fields completely eaten by locusts, their wives snatched away by death, and their children wandering aimlessly. Even with such memories Abu Safa still managed to recover his happier frame of mind. "In spite of everything," he insisted, "our generation was still happier than this spoiled one. Isn't it odd: you can be happy in the midst of deprivation, and miserable in times of plenty?"

At this point he paused. Obviously so many images were racing through his mind that he could not decide what to tell me first. He told me about his childhood love for Ghariba and how bitterly he had wept when she was married. He had watched her as a bride riding past the front of his house on a horse. He told me about Saba, Jamil al-Farah, Ibrahim al-Asad, and Shaykh Ibrahim al-Husayn. The shaykh, he told me, was a very generous man, and his wife insisted on offering hospitality to everyone who passed by the front of their house. Abu Safa told me that he had recently gone to see Shaykh Ibrahim's son, Mahmud, to ask a favor. Mahmud had refused even to discuss his request till they had eaten a dish of mutabbala.

Ah, Abu Safa, how delicious mutabbala is! True enough, we used to enjoy trivial things and think they were wonderful. Others may see our river as a brook, but for us it's a river. They may think our mountains are just hills, but for us they're mighty mountains, almost touching the sky. Is it any exaggeration to say that your son, Safa, the physician, treated a patient for several days in Washington without compensation because he knew the man was from Barshin, which is not far from Kafrun? You say you don't know when you started swimming. You're not exaggerating. I don't know when I started either. It was as if, like fish, we were born in the water. Is it strange that our friend, Said, who recently retired and has become crazy about fishing, has noticed that, whenever he feels really relaxed, memories of Kafrun come flooding back? The poetry he abandoned long ago is once again awakened inside him. Again he tells me that he spent his entire childhood and adolescence in Kafrun, so he knows it better than any of us. Just as a mother regrets the loss of a son at an early age, so he regrets emigrating and getting caught up in the details of a cold world. He recited (actually he virtually sang) a poem for me, written in 1942 after an encounter with his beloved at Shaykh Hasan Spring.

*Oh my love, morning veiled our souls;*
*Inclining to search, it found us,*
*The spring whispered to the blackbirds*
*Of our secret meeting, and they sang out our love.*
*This is he, the shaykh, calling us,*
*His garment—God bless him!—*
*A haven, sanctuary-like, to cover and protect us,*
*Spreading a veil over the shadow of our steps.*

Said stops singing, anxious not to drift back into his sorrows and lose control over feelings that he has kept buried inside him. Deep in his heart he realizes that the civilized world has robbed him of the grace of poetry, but he only blames himself. He writes of his sorrows, maybe his anger too—I don't know. He sings another stanza from an old poem of his:

*The spring wept out of love,*
*And the night grew ecstatic, then slept.*
*In our arms we cradled each other,*
*and our lips came together*
*in fervent kisses.*

*The morn woke and arose,*
*and proffered greetings to the shaykh.*
*A caressing breeze wafted*
*to the sides of our companions,*
*pressing our lips and*
*moistening our cheeks,*
*fragrance wafting to and from us.*

*Arise, beloved, and let us away,*
*for the morn has exposed our passion.*

Is it so strange that poetry should overwhelm the world of our friend, Said Jibrin, while he fishes at Potomac Falls? Or that, with no audience to hear, he should sing a stanza from a new poem he wrote in 1986 that links it to the old poem?

*O night, let me be!*
*You have disappointed me in love.*
*What you came to ask of me*
*I have lost years ago.*

We have lost so much, Said! That's why I still cling to memories of childhood, cherishing them like so many budding apricots and pomegranates.

Like a stallion I run in the mill-brook; like a fish or frog I swim in the river depths beneath the sycamore. With Zaki, Sabri, Ramiz, Badi', Badri, and Husni I swim naked in the water of al-Huma. Then, still wet, I put on my clothes again and go to see Hasan, Mahmud, and 'Abd al-Latif. Once I was shocked when Hasan climbed the ladder, caught a pigeon from a hole above the threshold, slaughtered and barbecued it, and then fed it to us, all without even asking his mother. To this very day, Hasan, I still feel guilty about slaughtering that poor innocent pigeon, even though I'm aware that it was intended as a generous gesture. Do you know what happened after that particular feast? I went down to Shaykh Hasan Spring and found a cluster of grapes in the water. I ate them all. Only later did I discover that your sister had left them in the spring to cool, so she could offer them to a dear guest you were expecting.

I run in the river, strutting like a defiant, proud steed just released from its saddle and reins. Water splashes to right and left, all over my face, chest, and shoulders. Water, water, and more water! In the beginning the earth was water, and so it will be again. I am with it at the outset when it gushes forth in springs. Like a waterfall I plunge toward deep valleys; across plains I flow and trickle down into the earth's belly and the pores of plants. I turn into vapor, travel the clouds—now white, now dark, causing thunder and lightning and teeming down as rain (O rain, secret source of fertility and birth!). The thirsty land absorbs me to quench its thirst, then I burst like a spring among rocks, like the Shaykh Hasan spring (O tender poet, poet of sorrows, Shaykh Hasan), or like al-Sheer spring (you haven of hawks, al-Sheer, you the unreachable!), or like the Karkar spring from which Nasim Massuh drank, thus becoming a popular poet and calling himself Nasim of the Spring.

I went down to the river, jumping from rock to rock, and climbed the sycamore tree that stretched over the water. I hunted fish and picked blackberries; my fingers were stained with their blood and mine. I hid behind a thick sycamore tree and watched a group of girls swimming. They didn't swim naked as we boys did, but as soon as their clothes got wet, their earthly goods burst forth, enveloped in a translucent mist. Oh, how beautiful is that which the body keeps hidden!

When I got to the Makhada River that day, I found a group of my friends swimming. I took off my clothes, and we had a diving contest. Some girls walked past at the Makhada crossing, but we did not cover our docile pigeons; quite the contrary, we hoisted them westward in their direction. The mother of one of the girls, who was carrying a bundle of corn on her head, yelled at us, "May God uproot the lot of you, you and your pigeons together! Behave, you scoundrels!" Had she known about my relationship with her daughter, she would indeed have pulled my pigeon out by its roots. A week earlier, I had been walking with her daughter in the fields to the west; we were talking about a mysterious scandal that had caused an uproar in the village. A man had caught his daughter sleeping with a young boy under a bay-leaf canopy. He gave her a severe beating. The lovely girl with whom I was walking alone in the fields asked me about it; she was wondering what the young boy and girl could have been doing. It was noon, the fields were empty, and it seems I decided practical application was better than theoretical explanation. So I sneaked the lovely girl into the thick, long rows of corn; and there we engaged in the necessary role-playing. In spite of my persistence we did not repeat the game later on. She was really scared. Thereafter, whenever we met by chance, each of us ignored the other. Perhaps she had discovered that my pigeon was not all that innocent, even at such an early age. I wonder, do you still remember things as clearly as I do? Even if I just happened to run across you today, I think I'd feel embarrassed. Would you blush just a little? God forgive us all, my little girlfriend. Will you get angry, I wonder, if you catch your daughter, who looks a lot like you, playing the same game? I don't have a daughter, so I don't know how I would act in such a situation. Oh, by the way, I can assure you that I've never mentioned your name to anyone, even though I sometimes find myself bragging about that beautiful, sweet adventure, as sweet as you were, you dream from the distant past. I've never told you before that we've often met in my dreams and played the love-game in very different guises, situations, and venues, benefiting from readings and experience I've acquired since that time. Once I dreamed that we made love high in a tree; another time under water. I was amazed that we could hold our breath for so long. There was still another dream that I've tried for ages to suppress. At school we had lots of religion classes. You came to me once in a dream in the guise of an angel with strangely colored wings. We played the game on the ground, high up in trees, and inside a cloud, then I went peacefully to sleep in the shadow of your angelic wings. We turned into glittering waters that met and parted, met and parted, in the shade of willows and sycamores and of white clouds reflected in the river.

Listen, I want to confess something and apologize. Twenty years later, I met you in a service-taxi, but I did not talk to you. I felt so sad and disappointed! That day I was taking a car from Tripoli to Safita, and you were sitting next to the driver with two small children. The driver asked you about your family and your brothers, so I knew it was you. Girlfriend of my youth, how much you have changed. Now you're fat and wrinkled, and your hair has turned gray. I felt sad. How can this happen while you're still young? I wonder, did they marry you off to an old man against your will, so you've neglected yourself to this extent? Why is it that women stop caring about their personal appearance once they get married and start their family life? I'm not saying you're wrong; I'm just wondering. Perhaps you had no other choice. I was afraid of reminding you who I was, in case it erased the distance between dream and reality. Following that encounter in the car, my imagination has erased the distance, and I dream no more. Once and for all the game has ended, to be replaced by the nagging sense of tragedy at the way women age while still young. Sometimes it occurs to me that you actually did recognize me, but pretended not to know me for much the same reason. I think I'm less lucky than my brother, who has not seen his childhood girlfriend since the time when he bribed her with gum. She went into the bay leaf canopy with him and revealed her lovely goods, a revelation as lovely as a summer morning in Kafrun. If only those old days would return, and we could go out to the fields before sunrise and pick figs, grapes, pomegranates, and red tomatoes!

After we had swum in the water of the Makhada and allowed our pigeons to fly west in the young girls' direction, I put my clothes back on and headed for the mill. The millstone was turning at a crazy speed, and I watched spellbound as the dark grains of wheat systematically fell to their fate and were transformed into white flour. The incredible noise started to get on my nerves, and I realized that conversation inside the mill was like a dialogue of the deaf. I went outside and stood by the old bridge over the waters of the Jaafura. The water was foaming and leaping like a group of ravenous tigers. Without taking my clothes off I go down to the water's edge; after a moment's hesitation, I suddenly jump into the middle and stand there defying its tremendous momentum. I laugh ecstatically, determined not to give in. My words disappear in the speeding current; up and up they rise, but they can't be heard over the roar of the water. I pull myself out of the water as it gushes like so many hungry tigers, then plunge in once again. I move toward the bridge, but this time the wild water knocks me over. I fall over and am carried downstream. I feel so happy. Taking off my clothes, I hang them up on the sycamore tree to dry. I lie on the pumice-stone, naked in the sun, pulse coursing. I surrender to the sun's rays and close my eyes. It's still a blazing hot day, and I blend with the light, the trees, white clouds, sun, sky, and the never-ending roar of the water. The harvest seasons have been good, and the mill never stops. Donkeys arrive with wheat from other villages and go back loaded with flour. I recover my own existence and resist any further blending. I long to stay this way, submitting and utterly taken, with no crisis on the horizon. How is it I can now feel hunger penetrating me, and so fast? How long ago did I digest the pigeons, grapes, and blackberries? I forget my own questions. I am like the water itself, traversing sinuous valleys as I plunge my way to the sea with an ecstatic freedom. There is no end, only eternal departure, and how wonderful it is, that eternal departure, with no beginning and no end! O crane, I think that you share this feeling with me. Are we then hostages to our own eternal habits?

My clothes are still damp when I put them back on. I rush to the orchards to look for Fahim, Salim, Jamal, Nayif, and Jihad. We pick ears of corn, then collect the dry branches and make a pile. I take out the stump of a desiccated berry tree from Elias al-Akhras's orchard, then go to borrow a flint and wick from him so we can start the fire and roast the corn ears. Elias was nick-named "al-Akhras" (the dumb) because from childhood he could neither speak nor hear. He was highly intelligent and had no real difficulty communicating with other people in the village. When he could not understand our gestures or read our lips, we used to trace words in the air with our fingers since that was how he had learned to read and write. Sometimes he would talk to me with his lips, and other times he used his fingers: "Why don't I see more of you?" he would ask. "Our field is your field. The grape clusters are shimmering like gold in the sun. Climb up vine and pick some grapes. Eat as much as you can and fill up a basket for your family at home. Your dear father was my friend—God have mercy on him. It is true that we had a fight one time over my uncle. I knew your father was strong and courageous, but I thought I was too. We met right here, where the stream divides. He soon threw me to the ground; I don't deny it. I was a stronger arm-wrestler, but he didn't arm-wrestle. He was bold and fast rather than strong, and never showed the slightest fear or hesitation. Even so, he never picked a fight with anyone unprovoked. He's the only one who ever beat me. Your father was fairly tall and thin, powerful and generous. Everybody loved him. At weddings he used to put on his boots, wrap his broad belt around his waist, fix his headdress and headband in his own unique way, fold up his handkerchief, and then take the lead in dancing the dabka. He was truly beloved."

"And you, Uncle Elias, are beloved too!"

"Thank you. After the fight we made up immediately; in fact, our friendship really began after that confrontation. Unfortunately, it did not last for long, as he died shortly thereafter. Nobody could believe that he'd died, and so quickly. Death at a young age is sharp-edged, like a flint. I've forgotten to get you the flint and wick."

I want you to know, Elias al-Akhras, that, as I stand here watching the Potomac Falls and myself from the edge of a high bluff, I can still remember you. I heard you got married and had children. It was only later I found out about the tragedy that befell you. I regret that I couldn't convey my condolences to you in person. Do you realize that, right until now, I still don't really know how to give condolences properly or how to settle down? Now I live far away, exiled and uprooted. No, no. Exile does not imply that I have no roots. Even though the branches of my life-tree reach out far and wide, my own are sunk deep into the soil. I feel that I will be seeing you soon. When we meet, we will not discuss your tragedy or mine. As long as there is love, we will manage to transcend tragedy, however great it may be.

All these memories had come bursting forth from within me, even though I imagined I had completely forgotten about them. Soon afterward I received some very sad news. Samir called me from Detroit. We had our usual conversation, but then he said, "Oh, by the way, Elias al-Akhras died." Alas, so we won't get to meet next time I visit Kafrun. I wish I believed in another life beyond this world, so I could console myself with the hope of meeting you there after a long life. As it is, I don't think we'll meet from now on. You, no doubt, believe there's another life, so you can be reunited with your son who was killed in the prime of his youth.

As far as I'm concerned, you may think that I don't remember any of these things. Believe me, I can recall them all with total clarity. How, and why, I've no idea. The village, its people, springs, hills, valleys, birds, roots, flowers, thorns, sadness, and joys, they've all taken root deep inside me. No one, nothing, can take them away from me. As the tree of my life withers, so another tree grows from its deep, deep roots.

# Descend, O Death

We move away from the edge of the bluff overlooking Potomac Falls and sit in an isolated spot. The angry roar of the river still drowns out all conversation. Closing my eyes I listen to the sound of the river, as though listening to storm music.

I look into my beloved's eyes, a long stare. "What's the matter?" she asks with a smile.

"Nothing," I reply, "nothing at all. I'm just trying to travel through your eyes."

Her smile widens as gradually she too returns from the dream world. Her smiling expression turns quizzical, then perplexed—all blended (or, at least, so it seems to me) with a certain mocking curiosity. "So, where were you?" she asks. "You certainly weren't with me."

"Nor were you with me."

"You definitely weren't in this world at all. You seem to be going through a state of delirium or insanity."

"It's a poetic state, I think. Poetry, ah poetry. Is there anything more splendid than the vast realm of poetry?"

"Music."

"They're the same thing."

"But you're somewhere completely apart from me. If you remember, we originally went out together to talk about our situation and what we can do about it."

"You're far away from me too; in fact, you're not yet back from your journey."

"I was wondering what'll happen to us when we're older. Will we stop loving each other? Will we be too preoccupied with our basic needs?"

She's thinking about my mother. I had already forgotten her. We had gone out in order to forget about her. "Do you have to remind me of her?" I ask somewhat angrily.

"She is an image of our own future."

"Do we always have to be thinking about our future?"

"No, we certainly don't. But, whether we like it or not, it's just one of several thoughts that crop up. Even so, it's still better to talk than keep things bottled up."

"That's true."

For a moment I said nothing, then I put my arm around my beloved's shoulders. "We'll never stop loving each other," I said. "We won't let ourselves go beyond the limits that would make us lose control of our own lives. I hope that we won't let ourselves do that."

"How will we know when we're close to the limit?"

"I hope we'll realize it. We didn't choose to be born, but we should at least be able to choose our own death."

At this point my beloved protested, "This is a weird conversation!"

"You're right!"

"Then again, we're always suppressing the most critical questions."

"We're living in an ephemeral, poetic world. As long as we are, I don't see why we have to revert to reality and critical analysis. Let's just enjoy it. How often in life do we flee the cycle of reality?"

She looks at me, and I notice a sarcastic smile brightening her face. "In your case," she says, "you should be asking how often you return to reality!"

"Dreams, reality, what's the difference? There aren't any borders between them. Maybe they're both aspects of a single truth."

"So what do you mean when you talk about the gap between dream and reality?"

"I don't mean splitting the truth."

"The truth?" interrupted my beloved. "What's the truth? Is there such a thing? If so, what happens to your notion of relative, conflicting truths? There is no absolute truth. Only transcendental idealists believe that."

"That's true, but then why do we keep going back to analysis?"

"Let's stop asking questions about our life."

Without even asking, I continued my journey into her eyes, moving in the direction of both past and future and inside the depths of the present. I won't ask her what she's thinking about. If she asked me what I'm thinking about, could I really tell her without some kind of sifting, censorship, or distortion? She too must have gone on a fantasy journey. I wonder, does she remember our first meeting as vividly as I do?

We listened to the clamor of the falls, and I continued my journey in the vast realm of her eyes.

"Do you remember the black hymn," I asked, "the one we learned in Ann Arbor in the early sixties during the heyday of the civil rights movement and opposition to the Vietnam War?"

In a subdued voice my beloved sang:

*Descend, O death, descend*
*Descend to Savannah in Georgia*
*To the depths of Yamakro*
*And search for sister Carolina*
*Who suffered in my vineyards.*

*She suffered the heat of days*
*And was exhausted*

And we finished it together:

*Descend, descend O death, carry her to me.*

"What brought that back now?" my beloved asks. "The civil rights movement was ages ago. Could it have been that beautiful black elevator operator?"

"Maybe it's my father's death and yours; the crane's death too, and the death of homeland and my mother as well."

"Was that what you were thinking about?"

"I found myself traveling back to my childhood in Kafrun."

"I was recalling the past too, but unfortunately, in light of the present."

"Why can't we rid ourselves of past and present?"

Without answering, my beloved started quietly singing another verse from the hymn. I tried to join in:

*Shed no tears, shed no tears,*
*Sister Carolina didn't die.*
*O husband, broken hearted, don't weep.*
*O broken hearted son, don't weep.*
*O girl, bereaved and lonely, you've wept enough.*
*She has only departed to her homeland.*

We stopped. I wonder, is death really a return to homeland? Where's my mother's homeland? I sing once again with my beloved who must have remembered another verse; she keeps singing warmly, and a smile shines in the sky of her eyes:

*She saw sweet death, she saw sweet death*

*Coming like a star descending toward the earth.*
*Death didn't frighten sister Carolina.*
*It was a friend she yearned to meet,*
*She whispered 'I am going to my homeland.'*

We took refuge in a tense silence. How does my mother envision death? As a lover, a savior, a star descending to earth? Does it scare her? Does she yearn to meet it? All I know is that she keeps saying that death is due and true. Maybe she feels that we want her to die and go to her rest. The one thing I know for sure is that she's still a past-master at the game of making me feel guilty.

Yesterday it was grapes she wanted. I told her we didn't have any at the moment. With that she lay down and closed her eyes. With her arms slumped to her sides, she trembled and told me she wanted to die. "I'm going to die, you know," she said. "If you don't fetch me some grapes, you'll be sorry."

I give a hearty laugh. Recalling her words now, I can laugh. But my beloved brings me back to reality. She takes me back to the bluff overlooking the falls so we can find out why a number of people are watching a young boy and girl. They are getting ready to climb down at a spot where there's a vertical drop to the river. It seems to be their hobby, especially the boy; they own the latest rock-climbing gear. They tie colorful ropes firmly to the trunk of a tree growing by the edge of the bluff and bend out a little to overlook the river below, just like the fig tree of al-Dahr in Kafrun. They must have been aware of the ever-increasing number of people standing around them, so they deliberately played the game of suspense. They inspected everything with obvious skill, all to increase people's sense of anticipation as they enjoyed the vicarious pleasure of watching a dangerous adventure in the making. Once they had checked the steep incline of the bluff several times from different angles, the girl decided to take the easiest way down via a safe route. At last, just when the crowd started getting impatient, the girl went down slowly and cautiously. She was followed by the boy, who descended rapidly. No sooner had they reached the bottom than everyone started applauding. I found myself clapping with everyone else, but my beloved was more restrained. From her perspective their sport was merely a frivolous adventure involving spoiled youth vainly trying to fill a vast void in their lives. I too thought to myself that we've all become too accustomed to taking the safe route and avoiding adventure; that is, until it's forced on us.

Suddenly and without any forethought, I found myself close to the edge of the bluff, searching for a safe way down. My beloved was yelling at me to turn back. Instead I headed for the sideways slope and started going down. I had no ropes or other technical support, but simply used what I'd learned during my childhood in Kafrun. I went down quickly and without hesitation, leaving no opportunity for my beloved or myself to persuade me to turn back. Fearlessly I made my way down toward the river, ignoring my beloved's cries in Arabic and an official notice warning of the danger of death. Once I had passed the point of no return, I paused at several points, but always managed to find a safe foothold or tree branch to cling to. This place wasn't any harder than the rocks of the al-Sheer Spring in Kafrun, or the Eagle's Nest, or the slopes of al-Sayida mountains. This is exactly what I used to do as a child, so why should I be scared? True enough, my cousin did fall once and crack his head open. All I had to do now was trust my childhood intuition. And that's how it turned out. The body's intuition never lets you down. I focus my vision and pay no attention to anything else. Step by step, I make my way down. I'm halfway there. Now it's become steeper, but there's no turning back. I move down in a zigzag. Now I'm three quarters of the way down. Going back is impossible. So I have to jump the last few meters to a flat rock.

I hesitate a moment, then I jump, bouncing like a ball as soon my feet touch the rock. I look upwards to reassure my beloved, but she remains motionless.

I move toward the edge of a rock slightly submerged in the river. There I sit, listening to the roar and watching the eddies. I turn my face ecstatically into the flying spray and breathe deep breaths, releasing all the pent-up tension within me. I spot a fallen tree that serves as a natural bridge to a rock planted firmly in the midst of waters that have run their course for thousands of years. Moving over to the tree-bridge, I make sure that it is secure, then without hesitation use it to cross over to the rock-island. There I find myself surrounded by clashing waves. I don't look upward, in case I see my beloved; I can no longer even hear her angry yells. Amid so much rushing water, I feel I am hearing Beethoven's ninth symphony. For the first time, I feel it is coming from within me, not from far away or from somewhere outside. From deep inside me it is born and wells up, enveloping me like a tornado. I cling to it and enter its belly, surrendering myself to its waves and losing myself in it. It carries me in different directions at the same time. We were united, and all separation came to a complete end. How wonderful was such total fusion!

*O my friends*
*Let us rid ourselves of sorrow*
*Let us sing together the ode to joy*
*In the shadows of soaring cranes*
*Let us sing of joy that rises from the depths of the earth*
*Let us open our chests to the air, laden with water*
*Waters. Waters. Again waters*
*In the beginning was water*

Suddenly I feel separated. I look up at my beloved and see her still anxiously waving at me to come back. A number of people have gathered around her. It's now I realize how stupid I've been. Am I out of my mind? What am I doing? What for?

I feel totally scared, unable to move. I can't go back even if I want to. Crossing that tree-bridge looks very dangerous. I must conquer my fear and go back, but I can't. The fear intensifies and turns into terror. I must conquer my fear. How? I can't. I yell at myself to calm down. Once again, I contemplate the rushing water, listen to sound of its headlong flow, and feel at one with the river's music. I recover my self-control, lie down at the rock's edge, and gaze at the water rushing furiously toward me like thousands of hungry tigers.

Once again pictures of the mill bridge in Kafrun come to mind. I approach without taking my clothes off. I approach, expose myself to the rushing water, and laugh in ecstasy as I refuse to give way. I sing, but my voice is lost in the roaring water. My voice gets louder, but it can't rise above the roar. I take off my wet clothes and stretch out in the sun on the pumice-stone under the big sycamore tree. My pulse is coursing, and I melt amid the roaring water and blazing sunlight. Above me hovers a big bird; it's an eagle. If only it were a crane! Like you, I traverse continents with no place to settle. I travel across the world, always in danger of being hunted down. Yes, I too have lost many of my feathers, but new ones have sprouted and now I can soar fearlessly over rivers in different continents. Oh, how I long to see the sun rising like a blazing amber over the glorious Nile as it stretches away like a green vein in the body of the desert.

From somewhere deep inside me I yell to my uncle Yusuf: At this very moment I'm thinking of you! Like my father and mother and the crane, you take my world by storm. You too are a unique crane. I'll never forget the day the flood almost washed you away. It seemed to swallow you up in death, but then the spirit's grace gave you strength to leap away and escape its clutches. You grabbed hold of your mule's halter as it was struggling to save its own life, a life as dear to you as that of Fahim and Said. It knew how to swim with the current, so it saved you. Around the fire we celebrated the way both of you had escaped. We ate walnuts, raisins, and pastries, and you fed the mule barley instead of hay. That day I listened eagerly to the stories my grandfather Salim told about other flood incidents, the like of which Kafrun had never known before and would never know again. The roots of the huge exposed sycamore tree in the fields to the west are eloquent testimony to that fact. You were saved, but you still lived long enough to witness the catastrophic death of your son, Said. To tell the truth, I put part of the blame on you, but you acted as best as you knew how. I can only share your grief. I remember the day you brought Said to Beirut; we were taking him to the hospital to have a malignant tumor on his knee treated. The doctor said that the tumor was cancerous; the leg would have to be amputated. You refused and took him back to the village. Later I heard that you went to the person whose cure for cancer involved burning the spot with an iron bolt. I can only imagine Said screaming as he felt the hot iron bolt on his knee and the smoke from his own burning flesh drifted up into his eyes. You had him burned him several times, but he did not get any better. On the contrary, his condition worsened. Finally someone, I don't know who, suggested to you that he spend a night on his own in Saint Elias's cave. Did you really carry him to Saint Elias's cave and leave him to spend the night there by himself? Did you forget all the terrifying stories about that cave? How many times had you told us stories about brave men who had accepted the challenge and gone to spend the night in Saint Elias's cave outside the village? Some of them emerged completely insane, while others were so scared that they wet their trousers. How could you have forgotten all those tales? How did you allow yourself to leave little tender Said in that cold dark cave? Of course, you found him dead next morning. Was that really the way it happened? I can't bring myself to believe it.

Now, as I sat on that rock amid the rushing waters of Potomac Falls, I felt very depressed. Had I brought myself to that rock the same way my uncle Yusuf brought Said to that cave? What madness was this? What stupidity?

Without even pausing for thought, I stood up and made my way across the tree-bridge back to the riverbank. I no longer felt scared because I badly wanted to be safe. Without glancing down I climbed up the rocks again. Once at the top, I had to face my beloved's anger. "Are you completely out of your mind?" she yelled. "You really are! Sometimes I don't understand what happens to you. What are you trying to prove?"

All I could think of saying by way of response was, "I don't know." She shook her head and walked quickly toward the car. I followed her, but only after taking another look back at the falls to bid them farewell. If only I could be transformed into a rushing, foaming river, adopt the shape of the air, embrace the rocks, or take off toward the sea with my arms wide open like the crane's wings! What was the point of Said's death? Why was the crane killed?

In spite of the danger of death, cranes still come in their normal season. Flock after flock, they soar in the vast expanses between the azure sky and the shadows of trees along the riverbank, immense, majestic, and proud. Hunters rush for their rusty guns. Within moments the sky is filled with shots as though war had been declared. Feathers float through the air. One by one the cranes crash to the ground and are grabbed by hunters who feel enormously proud of their extraordinary achievements; it's as though they are victors in some long-fought war. Why? Why? Why? Can you explain to me why?

I wake up from my fantasy journey safe and sound and hurry to catch up with my beloved. She refuses to look at me. I apologize, but she refuses to accept it. We continue our trip to the Shenandoah Mountains. She too is eager to climb to the summits and survey the world. Rather than continuing to flounder our way around in accumulated trivia, we want to visualize some form for it. We want to see this world spread out endlessly in every direction. We climb one summit after another; as one horizon disappears, another broader one comes into view.

My beloved tried to stay annoyed. After I had made several futile attempts to placate her, she finally decided to put her feelings into words. "Who told you that I want to witness you die tragically too?"

"Who said that I was looking for a tragic death?"

"So what was that crazy behavior all about then?"

"Our life is shallow."

"I tell you, there's no point in running away."

"Do you think I was trying to run away?"

"How else would you describe your behavior?"

"I don't know."

Together we ran away to Kafrun by way of the lofty green Shenandoah Mountains.

# The Longing for the Flute

I gaze at her, seeing my own face in hers. Perhaps she can see her face in mine. The world turns into a river. Everything is moving, growing, undulating, raging, and plunging. Currents toss us around, rising and falling with us, while their salt seeps deep inside us.

"I'll drive," I hear my beloved say.

"Why?"

"Don't I have the right?"

"Of course. But I want to know why now?"

"Because your stream of consciousness is in charge."

I wrap my arm around her shoulder. "Don't let it bother you," I say.

"But it does!" she interrupts firmly. "And when I'm around," she goes on, "I don't want you doing any more clownish stunts. Never again! Do you understand?"

"I understand."

We headed toward the Shenandoah, leaving behind us rituals of the masses and waterfalls in order to adopt those of forests and mountains. At this point I suddenly remembered the new cassette we had. "Did I tell you," I asked my beloved, "that Sami's sent me a tape of Nasim Massuh from Brazil? Unfortunately the recording isn't great, but the voice is the same one I knew in my childhood. Now I can critique his poetry, but I hate to assassinate the dream. I won't look at his poetry; I'll just listen. His voice is incredible, and he has a rare vitality to him. His spirit is like a wind blowing through ancient valleys. At the end of his life, he left the village and went to join his children in Brazil. He died in exile, still drinking arak and singing until his liver gave out."

With that, memories of the singer-poet who sang of longing for the flute came flooding back.

That night we stayed up with the moon till morning. I can no longer recall the occasion, but the Makhada was full. On the south bank a large number of village people had gathered around a table full of appetizers and arak. Nasim Massuh (or rather Nasim al-Nab, to use his preferred name) kept singing: ataba, mijana, ma'anna, and the dal'una. All around him people kept clapping, sighing, and repeating one chorus after another. On the other bank, another crowd, young folk from the cities and their friends gathered around George al-Humsi (and his name—someone from the Syrian city of Hums—suits his character) who was playing the oud and singing songs by 'Abd al-Wahhab, Farid al-Atrash and others, singers whom the people had started hearing on the radio at that time.

There was clearly some sort of contest going on between the two groups. People started to worry in case the celebration turned into a brawl. Of course, I had joined Nasim al-Nab's group and was annoyed by the screaming of the other group. But Nasim himself was not at all upset; quite the contrary, he was cheerful and self-confident, as brilliant as always. He sang from the depths of his heart, using a unique grating timbre that echoed the sentimental sound of the flute; when he sighed, the crowd sighed with him. Like the sun rising from behind the mountains to the east, his voice rose like some cloud that offers people welcome shade on a hot day:

*Sweet girl, show me the ways of love.*
*From the sweet moisture of your lips let me drink.*
*From the fount of your black eyes let me drink,*
*What charms are revealed by your lashes!*

Glasses and voices were raised in response. One man spread his arms as far as he could. "God bless you, Nasim al-Nab!" he yelled.

He continued with a strophe of mijana:

*O lofty peaks of our homeland*
*How refreshing is your air!*

And the crowd repeated after him:

*O lofty peaks of our homeland.*
*How refreshing is your air!*

Heads swayed in ecstasy, hands clapped. People from the other group joined ours. The circle widened and thickened, so I sneaked up to the front row. The table was filled with glasses of arak and appetizers. I remembered how hungry I felt, and yet shyness kept me rooted to the spot. Nasim gestured to me, and I walked hesitantly toward him. Dipping a piece of tomato in salt, he offered it to me and sat me down alongside him. I blushed shyly, but felt proud; how I wished my young girlfriend could be there to see me. I don't know why I thought of her at that particular moment; I don't think I needed to prove anything to her. I had definitely already proven myself to her in the cornfields, so perhaps I just wanted her to share my tremendous happiness.

From deep within him Nasim al-Nab sighed once more, and his voice came echoing forth:

*My love, bring your strings and oud*
*And to your friends sing your promises.*
*O poet, life has tuned you and your oud*
*To the sound of the nay and the plaint of the flute.*

Again sighs were heard. After downing a glass of arak, he went on with a strophe of mijana. As he sang, he turned to look at a beautiful gypsy woman sitting next to him:

*Fold your tents and move to our mountains.*

With the crowd she repeated:

*Fold your tents and move to our mountains.*

Clicking his glass against hers, he sighed and put his hand on her shoulder.

*Were you to spend summer in the peak of our mountain,*
*We would offer you our hearts.*
*Fear has no place in our midst*
*For our spears chase the heels of the enemy.*

Everyone was yelling from their innermost being, so he gave us another strophe of mijana:

*But for love,*
*Your father would not be my in-law.*

As the crowd repeated the strophes, they all clapped. He stood up and clapped with them, moving from one side of the table to the other and encouraging everyone to join in the song:

*Our tradition is to honor the guest,*
*No matter what afflictions may befall us.*

The crowd repeated this stanza too, so he sang it a third time until he was totally wrapped up in it. He went on.

*We ate mannah and drank wine,*
*And still your heart is so hard.*
*This time we'll fill the jars,*
*And drink from our winery.*

The crowd picked up the refrain with relish, while he kept clapping along with them and moved deftly between the groups.

*Our tradition is to honor the guest,*
*No matter what afflictions may befall us.*

He moved on to another strophe, one that the gypsy woman particularly enjoyed:

*Riding horses is our custom,*
*We target our enemy with disgrace and woe,*
*We do not fear in day or night*
*Or when the dawn breaks . . .*

And no sooner had they repeated it than he added another:

*The armor is of chains, my love,*
*Woven of David's thread.*
*We shepherd the lamb and the wolf*
*And compose verses all night,*
*Till the cock crows*
*And the moon cleaves the darkness.*

Once again applause is heard, and still more people from the other group join the circle. Nasim gestures to the shepherd to play on his double-reed flute. He leaps into the middle of the circle, while young men and women form themselves into a semicircular dabka.

I find myself eagerly watching the scene. Next to me is my little girlfriend who has suddenly arrived. I teach her the steps of the dabka, while she teaches me the secrets of love so early in life.

The shepherd and young folk started getting tired, so once again they turned to Nasim al-Nab. He put his hand on his cheek and without pause let out a languid sigh:

*I belittle myself while you boast.*
*I cool my temper, but you flare.*
*I sheath my sword, but you draw yours*
*And strike fear into enemy hearts.*

He continues with a strophe of mijana:

*Soar, my wings, soar up high,*
*Then land at my beloved's home.*

The singing goes on and on, late into the night. Like a feeling of numbness it penetrates all the way to obscure hiding places deep inside the soul. At just the right moments, Nasim al-Nab moves between the different realms of ataba, mijana, and zajal. Once again he gazes at the beautiful gypsy woman and sings:

*You can enchant me, young or old*
*You can restore me to my youth*
*You can make me fight a war and*

*Triumph over enemies*
*You can make me melt like a candle*
*And at the shrine you can burn me like incense*
*You can reunite me with my loved ones*
*Or keep my lover from me*
*You can make me an absent moon*
*And in the morning you can make me rise*
*You can make me melt like snow*
*And again make me freeze*

The singing went on and on until arak had numbed the mind and eyes grew heavy. Once Jamil had wrapped his arms around the poet and taken him into his house, the gathering broke up. Some of us children stayed by the river waiting for the moon to disappear. We played a game called "Gather the Feather" and danced the dabka. Our bare feet pounded the ground defiantly, and our handkerchiefs made circles on the face of the sky with ecstasy and pride. Before morning could slink its way in, I went over to the hammock that my father had made out of bayleaf branches. The moment my head touched the pillow, I fell asleep.

# Death in Exile

When the cassette came to an end, my beloved said that, even though he certainly had a beautiful voice, his poetry was nothing special. She wanted to hear some classical music, but I still wanted to listen to the sound of the reed playing; that way, we would stay in the realms of longing for the flute. She had her way, but that did not manage to distract me from my musings. Silently I addressed Nasim's spirit. I expressed my gratitude to him, my sadness at his death in exile, and my sorrow that, when he had passed by my house to bid me farewell, he had not found me there.

I thanked him for this particular verse of ataba. In my memory it's forever linked to my own father's death, so I used to recite it over and over again in a doleful tone that almost made me cry.

*The day of your departure I wept and grieved.*
*My heart is a rock, scored by the chisel of your death.*
*Were your shade to visit, I would greet it*
*with emotions pure as dew.*

I tell you, Nasim al-Nab, that's your most beautiful poem, but you are yet more beautiful than your poems. You may have died, but the legend lives on. I wonder, is that why you refused to publish your poetry or record your voice? The recording I have must have been made in secret, since I'm sure you knew intuitively that truth would kill the legend. We will have to make do with the few manifestations of your truth that we have left. We love you now just as we did in childhood. I am proud of the verses you once wrote for me when you didn't find me at home; you put them in the notebook that contained my very first short stories.

Nasim al-Nab's Bouquets for Halim: zajal strophes

*O patient, noble, all-knowing God,*
*Hear the prayers of the miserable and exhausted Nasim,*
*From the high dome of your heavens grant your imagination,*
*So my young friend Halim may surpass Khalil Gibran.*
*My God, I have none but Thee;*
*Thou art the Wise, the All-knowing, the Merciful.*
*Thou are the All-wise; give him Thy wisdom.*
*Thou art the teacher, and we know Thy message.*
*Make Halim to sit beside Thy throne,*
*So we may follow him and see his straight path.*
*So we may follow and read stories and fables*
*He has written whenever bells ring in schools.*
*Even when birds in cages chirp their songs,*
*They will be chanting the hymns of Halim.*

Nasim al-Nab, you make me feel so embarrassed! Till now I've kept these bouquets of verses hidden. I'm publishing them here because they are fragrant bouquets from you. I realize full well that they have nothing to do with me, nor do they really match the rest of your poetry as I recall it. For me writing is not a contest. I realize that there are zajal competitions, like arm-wrestling and fencing. I can tell you that it was under Gibran's influence that I started writing; he was the beginning of the road, but I chose a different one. Nasim, you know I'm not religious; I am not in quest of paradise, nor do I believe in the existence of a straight path, but rather in intersecting lines. However, I do believe that birds sing in their cages; we all chirp inside our own cages. We want to escape from those cages, fly away to open spaces, soar over valleys and mountain tops, and traverse horizons, all in order to die before our wings are broken and to remain a legend. Nasim, did you ever sing of the crane? Like him we wander forever and we die; from him we have learned the art of soaring and moving in formation. He and trees, rivers, and mountaintops, they are our companions.

O Nasim, I'm afraid that, by recording these little truths from your ocean, I have participated in the assassination of the legend. Why do I insist on publishing them? I don't know. Forgive me. If only I could let people hear the sound of your voice, maybe they'd forgive me my sins. This year I visited al-Nab. I was anxious to put a bunch of flowers on your grave, but I couldn't find it. Nasim al-Nab, "Nasim of the Spring," in what realm of the vast land of Brazil have they buried you? Can springs be buried?

It all makes me feel very sad; I almost start crying, something I haven't done for ages. I thought I was beyond that phase. To feel so powerless! For you to be lying in a damp pit alone, with no promise of salvation; that breaks my heart. My mind, chest, and stomach, I feel pain in all of them. We are tired of this migration. Your body lies in exile in South America, and here I am in North America. O Nasim al-Nab, if only we could wash our faces, you and I, in the waters of the Shaykh Hasan spring! When the crane comes, we must be there to protect it from the hunters' rifles.

Yesterday I read a strange tale. An idealistic American girl went to a lake in the middle of a forest to defend ducks and geese from hunters who drag away the birds they kill, leaving a trail of blood in the snow. She went over to the hunters and calmly talked to them about the birds' beauty and innocence and the way their numbers were diminishing year by year. When she finished, one of the hunters told her she was breaking the law; if she didn't stop bothering them, he would demand her arrest. She refused to stop, saying that she had the right to defend the birds just as they did to kill them. The hunters called the police. They came at once, arrested the girl and put her in handcuffs. She was informed that she had broken a law punishable by a fine of five hundred dollars or ninety days imprisonment. So, Nasim al-Nab, defending birds is prohibited! Idealists are not allowed to express their opinions in a way that bothers hunters. Have you ever heard of a law prohibiting protests against killing? I can assure you that this winter that American girl will be back at the lake in the middle of the forest, asserting her right to protest and demanding that this unjust law that protects the armed against the unarmed be annulled. We don't have laws; we have rulers.

Listen, I need to escape this abyss of sorrow. I strive to soar in your realms. Now I'm leaving the inferno. Deep inside I silently repeat the mijana verses that the crowds from our village and neighboring ones would often repeat after you:

*O lofty peaks of our homeland*
*How refreshing is your air!*
*Long be the time*
*That brings us all together.*
*But for love,*
*Your father would not be my in-law.*
*Soar, my wings, soar up high,*
*Then land at my beloved's home.*

Forgive me, Nasim al-Nab, I beg you! There's something else as well. I'm glad to be able to speak to you directly. I am jealous of that gypsy woman; the verses you composed for her are nicer than the bits of zajal you wrote in my notebook. Even so they're still better than those first short stories of mine that I'll never publish. I can't understand how you neglected to sing a poem to the crane, that one that in all primeval innocence used to cross the peerless Kafrun sky.

# Reading in the Clouds

The two of us meander our way through narrow, winding paths in the Shenandoah Mountains amid dense, colorful forests. The radiant, harmonious colors are so spectacular that we can't make up our minds: should we hurry on and discover yet more variations of color, or sit down and try to take in the ones in front of us? They lead us wherever they want, and as fast as they want. Trees of red, wine, green, and yellow together, gold, cranberry, burgundy, orange, sand, crimson—incandescent colors, radiant, warm, cool, wavy, loud, still, interweaving, pure, filtered, withered, vibrant.

We meander through forests, pausing to watch fearless deer that have grown accustomed to people. As we approach them slowly, they prick up their ears and open their eyes wide. I tear off a piece of a fresh branch and offer it to a deer that approaches us with its two fawns. I move two steps closer, but she doesn't run away. I move still closer. Stretching its head, it nibbles at the branch, but doesn't try a second time. My beloved remembers she has some peanuts; she puts some in her palm and offers them to the gazelle. We hold our breath, amazed that it could be that simple to extend a bridge across valleys of fear and doubt.

We continued our walk to the summit of Stonyman Mountain, stopping occasionally to contemplate a color, an animal, a unique tree, a scene, or a view. After a lengthy climb we eventually reached the top, exhausted. Once again we found ourselves looking out across a broad landscape that grabbed us from within in order to immerse us in thoughts that transcend all usual dimensions.

As the world's burdens fell away, we found ourselves transformed into birds, deer, and trees of fascinating colors; into swaying leaves and a sun masked by cool, transparent clouds roaming freely across the broad expanse in all four directions in pursuit of their personal whims.

We sat down on a big rock-cleft overlooking a limitless world. Is the universe limitless? What lies beyond millions of years of light? How can there not be any limits? Can there be anything with no end? Does space end? Does time? Where's the beginning? Is it conceivable for there to be no beginning? Where's the end? Using the same logic, can we conceive of there being no end either? Perhaps it's the mind itself that has limits, beginnings and endings, not the universe.

This time my beloved has sat down beside me at the edge of the cliff. "When I was a child," I tell her, "I used to climb al-Sayida Mountain. I'd look at the edges of the distant world and try to reach the sky. But, when I got close to the top, it would always elude me. I used to clamber up the mountain, hoping to get a glimpse of the sea, but it was always enveloped in clouds and fog. On Mount Sa'ih thick oak trees kept the universe completely concealed from me, so I used to sink with the roots into the veins of the earth."

"You're a prisoner of your own comparisons. Forget about Kafrun. These days it's the only reference point for everything in your imagination. The beauty you see in front of you deserves to be appreciated in its own right. Every beauty is special; every experience of beauty needs to be special too, something unique in itself. Start your relationship with these beautiful scenes here and on their own terms."

"Easier said than done."

"As long as you insist on making Kafrun your point of reference, you'll never be able to establish new relationships, nor will you be able to see any other type of beauty. If you were being fair, your comparisons would force you to reconsider. Just look at this view: Kafrun has no beauty to match this."

"Each one has its own particular beauty."

"Just admit the truth. Liberate yourself from such a subjective attitude and all its accompanying baggage!"

"The subjective part can't be changed. What you call 'accompanying baggage,' I term roots. That's why I still adore weeping willows; not just because its tears fall into the river and make circles that fold into each other, nor simply because, when the tips of its dangling branches are swayed by the breeze, they draw a series of eyes on the water's surface. No, I also love the weeping willow because it bends down to its roots and reverts to itself. It's just like me: as I get older, my branches also revert to my roots."

"You're going to end up focused on the past."

"God forbid! There are different modes of identity; some are rigid, others dynamic. Even so, I still can't free myself from the weeping willow that has taken root in my soul."

"And what about the subjective? You are proud of Kafrun's beauty; Americans are proud of America's beauty."

"They have the absolute right to feel proud. They're right."

"They came to the New World from various fringes of the old world and built an advanced society. They built a new society because they had started a new life unburdened by heritage and institutions, especially the ones that go back to eras of ignorance, poverty, and oppression. They uprooted themselves from their former societies and never looked back; that way, they could really start afresh. Of course, they couldn't free themselves completely from all aspects of their past history. They arrived hungry, and the new situation generated a greed in them. There were countless opportunities before them, and opportunism spread. They are a manifestation of the first stages of colonial imperialism. What they did to Native Americans and then to blacks is a historical disgrace."

"Not only that, but these days they're completing the tradition of European expansionism so as to oppress and dominate the world. You're right. These vast expanses of fertile land did generate further greed. Heading west was an act of exploration, but it was also an invasion with guns, one that showed no control or restraint. They drew borders on borderless terrain, then declared, 'This is my personal property,' and wrote signs saying 'No trespassing.'" As a result, they killed Native Americans twice: once with bullets, the second time by giving them a negative image in order to justify the killing. They depicted the victim as a backward and barbaric aggressor, whereas the actual murderer was an ambitious, harmless, culturally advanced, and devout pioneer. Native Americans are still being hounded and encircled to the point of extinction. Once the Americans had created a strong society, they turned their attention to the rest of the world, using exactly the same procedures they had used earlier in the move to the American West.

These days it's the Third World they're killing twice. Their relationship with their land, Native Americans, blacks, the Third World, and even space itself, is based on principles of oppression, domination, expulsion, siege, and exploitation. At the moment we're at the climax of this phase. They used to draw a particular image of Native Americans and then blacks, and now they're doing the same thing with the Third World. Thus the current and forever-smiling president of the United States can divide the world into two parts, the barbaric and the civilized, and use that as a basis for justifying aggression and murder. It's one of the great ironies of history that he considers himself civilized."

"You're oversimplifying things."

"Maybe. But every time I try to reconsider my convictions, I find yet more supportive evidence."

"You should open your heart to all types of evidence."

"Believe me, I'm trying."

"You may be trying, but you're not succeeding."

"The one thing that I can't overlook is the linkage I see between the American obsession with diet and Third World hunger. Your father—God be merciful to him—saw clearly that all the world's rivers pour into the American ocean. His own simple intuition told him so."

"You know he used to brag about that."

"True, but what's important is that he saw it all clearly. His own attitude is something else."

"His attitude is important too. He saw America as a land of opportunity and had to suffer a great deal in order to bring his family over."

"That's true too. But can we really ignore this linkage between greed in America and hunger in the Third World? America dominates the world economy. Its limitless greed drives it to exploit the globe's resources and squander its energies."

"What you're describing is the linkage of strong and weak in every time and place, including the Third World. The ruling classes there are even greedier and more overindulged."

"Absolutely. Greedy people over there are allied with the same group here."

"The weak are splintered. All the most cruel and futile wars are fought by the weak among themselves and against each another. There remains the question as to why we're living here and not there!"

"As you well know, my criticism of my own homeland is even harsher."

"Why do we have to have this conversation now? Let's just enjoy this beauty and forget the world's cruelty. Surely you don't have another sermon, do you? Say it now and get it over with. I don't want to keep going back to this same topic every few minutes. Empty your barrel. Why did you sidestep the question?"

I gave a coy laugh, fully aware that I had indeed avoided the entire issue. I was actually thinking about something I had been meaning to discuss with her for some time.

"I'm sorry," I replied hesitantly, "I'll change the subject. A thought just occurred to me, and I'd like your opinion."

"Just one more thought."

"Just one, I promise."

"Go ahead then. Enough boring stories."

I paused to collect my thoughts. "For some time now," I said, still hesitating, "I've been thinking that in American society there's a strong tendency to underline the importance of having 'fun' or having 'a good time.' But the whole thing involves 'fun' that's actually devoid of any genuine happiness. This is a 'fun' society without any real happiness. It's a 'fun' society in another sense too: Americans are always asking how to do something and not why. The word 'why' ends its function in childhood and the word 'how' takes over. How to get rich? How to succeed? How to enjoy sex? How to court your wife? How to be happy? How to change the car's oil?"

"Have you finished presenting your idea?"

"Yes, I finished a while ago."

"Thank God! Do you yourself always ask why? Do Arabs ask why? Just imagine how many restraints and taboos Arabs have!"

"A huge number, impossible to number."

We looked again at the mountain slopes, the blended colors of leaves, green plains, and white clouds in the far west assuming provocative shapes. I recalled the crushing weight of the past and the burden of morality. I found it all very distressing. In spite of the distances involved, I felt scared.

"When I was young," I told my beloved, "we used to sit in front of grandfather's house at the top of the hill, watching the cloud formations to the west and asking each other what patterns we saw. "I see a lion wrestling a tiger," Grandfather would say. "I see a little girl filling a jug," Grandmother would continue. "'I see a prancing stallion that has thrown his rider," would be my contribution, and Aunt Fahida would chip in with, "I see a field of cotton," and so on. As the clouds assumed new patterns, we would read their alphabet all over again. Now I realize that we were projecting ourselves on the clouds and viewing them with our inner eyes, ones we didn't even know we had. Let's read the clouds of America. What do you see in them?"

"I see a single, solitary cloud."

"I can see a moving map that shows the way land and sea come together."

"I can see a girl being chased by two young men."

"Where?"

"Over there in the shadow of that black cloud."

"I can see a naked woman with three breasts."

"I can see a white bear."

"I can see a black bear. I think it's going to rain. What do you say we go back?"

On the way down we looked for deer, rabbits, and chipmunks, all the while steering clear of dense thickets where we might run into a fierce bear. All this was accompanied by a special internal quest.

"Do you want to hear my latest dream?" my beloved asked. "I've been trying to remember it all morning."

"So now we've moved from reading clouds to reading dreams?"

"It was reading clouds that reminded me of my dream. They are always very unclear, more vague than clouds. I forget them quickly."

"Your dreams are always interesting."

"They're annoying too. Last night I dreamed that I was going to sing a recital in a large hall, though I knew I wasn't ready and didn't even know the words of the song. I thought of inventing my own special words and tricking the audience so as to make some money. I asked the pianist to play and started singing, 'I could have danced all night.' Although my voice sounded better than I had expected, I couldn't think of the appropriate words. The audience started to leave, and I soon found myself alone. I kept on singing and began to come up with the words; I was amazed at how beautiful and expressive they were and how my voice had improved."

"The other people represent censorship. There are masks because others are there. What an amazing dream!"

We went overboard in interpreting her dream. Half serious and half joking, I accused her of loving wealth. I noted that in one respect she seemed anxious to please others, while in another she still preferred loneliness and freedom.

I did not give her the chance to defend herself. "Now let me then tell you about my latest dream," I said.

"I know, you dreamed that you were flying?"

"No, not this time. Yesterday I dreamed I'd quit my exhausting job."

"Your job's exhausting?" she interrupted. "What about mine?"

"Don't interrupt. I forget my dreams so easily. I dreamed I quit my job and swam to a distant island looking for desert stallions that roam freely over the wide world. While I was swimming, I was afraid a shark would come up and take my leg off. As long as I was swimming, I felt scared. I was battered by raging waves and found myself being pulled away from the island instead of toward it. But I carried on swimming. The shark moves in. I close my eyes in surrender, waiting for it to devour me, but it doesn't even touch me or swallow me up. I'm amazed. I open my eyes again and look back over my shoulder, amazed that it has simply disappeared. I keep swimming toward the island. When I get there, I scale a hill and survey the vast plains below. Suddenly I spot a herd of desert stallions roaming in the wide-open country. I watched them charging aimlessly in different directions, shamelessly copulating, racing without bothering whether they win or lose. For a long time I watched them, feeling completely content. I've no idea how the dream ended."

"You must have discovered your lost life in it."

"I think I realized in my dream that I've been domesticated. I started invoking memories of the young stallion I once was in Kafrun, when I used to run through creeks and streams and water splashed to right and left, soaking my face and hair."

"There must be some connection between the dream you had and the news story we saw on television the day before yesterday, the one about wild stallions being chased in Wyoming so they could be caught and delivered to cowboys for taming or slaughtering."

"Yes, there must be a connection. It annoyed me to see them using a helicopter to chase the stallions till they were exhausted. Then they captured them and delivered them as bounty to the cowboys, those grandsons of Western pioneers."

Silence. My beloved and I could not think of anything else to say. With that, it occurred to me that silence was also linked to this dream-nightmare I had had.

"Let me tell you the latest joke I heard," I said, anxious to change the mood.

"Do you have any jokes left that you haven't told me many times before?"

"I have told you this one before, but you didn't laugh. So instead let me tell you a funny story from my life."

"It had better be good. Go ahead."

"When I was little," I began immediately, "maybe five or six, my father sent me to Abdullah Nassar's shop to buy a kilo of barley for the mule. I fell down on the way home, and barley was scattered all over the ground among the pebbles and soil. I was scared, so I picked up some of it and buried the rest in the ground. I went home, glancing nervously in every direction. When my father lifted the bag of barley, he looked surprised and started weighing it. Without pausing to question me, he took the bag and headed angrily for Abdullah's shop. I disappeared. When I came home later, I felt really scared. I learned that my father had put the blame on Abdullah. The latter had looked surprised, but had nevertheless apologized and given him another kilo with an extra handful."

"Didn't you tell your father the truth?" my beloved asked me disapprovingly.

I wanted to say that I had, but I found myself saying, "No."

"You coward!"

"Domesticated, if you will. That's why I never forgot that incident; it'll stay with me forever. I rarely forget my sins. Do you remember yours?"

"I can't remember any of them. I must be a sinless woman."

"So I married a pure woman then!"

That made her laugh long and hard. I felt like asking her why she was laughing like that and even to inquire about some of her sins, but I did not dare. For a while we walked together in silence, each one of us absorbed in our thoughts. Associations of all kinds were rampaging through my mind, although I had no idea how or why they were generated or how they were linked. Images from the past that I thought I had completely forgotten were suddenly revived within me, just as plants break through the earth's surface on a sunny day after a heavy downpour of rain.

As long as we are talking about sins, I can remember one occasion when I pushed my sister off a swing that my mother had set up for us inside the house. My sister started crying, but, as soon as my mother took a pot of lentil soup off the fire and put it on the ground, she stopped bawling. As my mother went about other household tasks, my sister sat by the pot of soup, watching the steam rise. I have no idea how I came to lose control of the swing, but I bumped into my sister again. She fell toward the pot and put her hand in the hot soup. My mother came running. As she was wiping the hot soup off my sister's arm, her skin started peeling off as well. My mother carried her outside, crying and weeping, looking for someone to help. Even now, I can still see my sister's skin in my mother's hand; fortunately the burn did not leave any permanent mark.

We look at the tree colors and collect some leaves as they fall to the ground like crane feathers floating hesitantly on the breeze. Leaves—yellow, red, wine, grape, sand, crimson, golden—all falling deathlike in the world of tired people. Leaves—radiant, blazing, resisting the fall, and swaying in the air until they gently touch the earth. Might human death be like that of autumn leaves?

# Makhul and Askess

Like autumn leaves and crane feathers, my father resisted the fall. Ever since that moment, I have been haunted by his fall. Whenever I hear the sound of his body tumbling, I refocus my thoughts and try to visualize him.

He had a thin face, the color of burnt honey. I especially recall his pronounced features, his expressions, and his deep eyes. His bamboo-like height was probably closer to tall than average. I also recall that he used to wear loose pants, a headdress, a headband, boots, and a wide belt. He was a master of the dabka dance. After tying and braiding his handkerchief, he would take the lead. He used to shake it so that it turned quickly and gracefully, like a fan, a sword, or a rod. From early childhood the dabka has always been engraved in my mind as a popular dance, one in which cooperation—hand to hand, shoulder to shoulder, competition, challenge, and individuality—all blend into one. Here freedom of movement and friendly rivalry are fused in a complete harmony. So thanks to you, Zaki Nasif, for bolstering these initial impressions in my memory.

Over the years I have heard a great deal about disputes involving my father. My mother and others from our village and neighboring ones have said that he was bold and without fear.

Everyone has assured me that he never instigated the conflicts he was involved in; people liked him, and he liked them. Personally, I can only recall witnessing two of his fights. One holiday, just as he was about to sit down and have lunch with a guest, someone came by and gave him the disturbing news that a fight had broken out on the mountain between his brother, Jamil, and Gharib al-Berber, who had several of his relatives with him as backup. I stood there watching as my father put his dagger in his wide belt, picked up his mace, and left. I followed him to the scene of the fight and watched from a distance. Since then, I've often wondered if my excuse for always watching fights from a distance was that, when I fight, words are my only weapon. Even so, I actually had to fight some real battles of my own, all of which ended in my favor. In that particular fight my father didn't even approach Gharib, but took on the strongest of his relatives. However, other people intervened and prevented my father from getting near him. I still remember what the relative's daughter, a friend of mine who was standing next to me, said in a censorious tone: "Your father's out to kill mine!" She was very pretty, so I didn't ask her why her father had come to help Gharib al-Berber against my father and why he had beaten up my uncle.

I remember the second fight just as well as the first. It happened when my Uncle Jawdat was assaulted, though I don't know what caused it. All I remember is my grandfather coming to our house in a rush. "I no longer have any children," he yelled. "People can attack us and get away without losing a single hair from their head."

As soon as my father understood what had happened, he rushed away armed with his dagger and mace. This time no one could stop him. He sought out three of the assailants and hurled them to the ground; that was enough to end the fight and bring about a reconciliation. Soon afterward my grandfather showed up and faked annoyance at his children, ordering them back to the house.

My father was always a vigorous presence when it came to dabka dancing, fights, singing, and making friends both inside and outside the village. Whenever I traveled to any of these villages, people honored and loved me because of my father's good reputation. They always told me that he had an overwhelming presence, one that inspired fear, respect, and love.

I clearly remember my father giving us something special every time came home from work. He never came home empty-handed. He would tie the mule to the China tree, take off his headdress and headband, shave, and fix himself a glass of arak. My mother would prepare the mezze for him, which invariably included a head of shanklish crushed with olive oil, a head of onion, and a flat loaf of Arabic bread, the color of his face. In summer the mezze always included cucumbers and tomatoes.

My mother told me that once she made the mistake of giving my father a loaf of bread not made of pure wheat. He had torn it up and fed it to the mule. "Where on earth did you get this bread?" he had asked. My mother had to explain that our neighbor, Sitt Zahiya, had borrowed a loaf of wheat bread but the one she had given back was mixed grain bread; my mother had not felt able to turn it down. Sitt Zahiya came from an upper-class family that owned the village mill; she used to give my mother advice on savings. On one occasion my father overheard her giving my mother advice.

"Dear Matron of Honor," he commented, "what is the point of this life? Tomorrow we'll all be dead anyway!"

Behind this hidden tension in the relationship there may well have been a desire on Sitt Zahiya's part for us to remain the way we were, at least symbolically. However, my father had other ideas and insisted on asserting both his own dignity and his right to transcend our family's current circumstances. When the effects of this tension became clear, both sides made an effort to hide it so that their mutual ties and interests would remain unimpaired.

My father's refusal to take her advice seemed to be linked to the way he addressed her with the wedding-phrase "Matron of Honor." For her part, she maintained that she only wanted the best for us and was offering her advice out of concern. And that's the way things remained.

My father worked as a muleteer, transporting much-needed goods and stones between villages in the region. Just as I can now travel between Washington, New York, Boston, Detroit, Chicago, San Francisco, Portland, and Austin; between America and Europe, the Maghreb and the Levant; and between south and north, so did my father ply between the villages of Kafrun, al-Mashta, Safita, al-Drikish, Marmarita, Mishtaya, Barshin, Mharda and Skilbiya. The names of other villages so often repeated by my father are also engraved in my memory: Uyun al-Wadi, Juwaykhat, Rabah, Akrab, Masayif, Bdada, Ayn al-Jurn, Haba, al-Yazdiya, Habb Nimra, and others. I remember too that he used to travel to Akkar; as he currycombed his mule, he would sing, "Mount Akkar, mountain of snow. . . ." Some of my uncles plied the same trade, and today their children still transport goods between the same villages in pickup trucks; now they've added Homs, Hama, Tripoli, and Tartus to the list.

"He had a wonderful voice," I tell my beloved.

"Who?"

"Oh, I was just thinking about my father."

"You can still remember his voice?"

"I think so. My brother's voice is just like his. I can still remember one particular night with absolute clarity. It was a cold and rainy evening, and Makhul came to visit us. In those days, who was there who didn't know Makhul? He had a big, unusually shaped head; he was ugly, short, rotund, poor, lonely, weird, and ostracized. He worked as a second- or third-class servant for my godfather, Faiq. As children that's all we ever knew about him. We didn't know where he came from or who his family was, although we'd heard talk that he was related to Yusuf's mother (the same Yusuf who was village champion in basin-stone lifting). He had no father, sister, or brother, and naturally he had no wife or children either. Who would agree to marry Makhul? He was like a dry branch cut off a tree in some unknown spot. Such was his lot in life, and as a result he was the butt of jokes and a village outcast. We used to chase him down alleys, yelling "Fathead Makhul" or "Snotface Makhul," then run away when he started throwing stones at us. We chased cats and dogs as well, especially when they were mating. Do you know that it's very difficult for mating dogs to separate?"

"No, I didn't know. But why were you all so mean?"

"I don't know. I keep asking myself the same question. On my recent visit to Damascus I was wandering through the Hamidiya Market looking for an old mother of pearl inlaid mirror for you. I saw children chasing and mocking a blind woman. 'Halima,' they kept yelling, 'Halima!' I asked a vendor why they were harassing the poor woman. 'Because we're an ill-mannered society,' he replied in exasperation. I was struck both by his forthright answer and his harsh verdict."

I have always felt guilty about hunting birds even in their nests. While I've kept such memories repressed till now, I find them clashing with my feelings about the crane. I feel embarrassed about disclosing them. Yet that is exactly what we used to do. Whence comes such viciousness? I'll never forget the pigeons that Hasan slaughtered. On one occasion I ate barbecued pigeon in Alexandria. Sometimes I blame myself for doing so, but when I'm too harsh on myself, I remind myself that most people eat animal meat. What boundaries separate vicious behavior and sheer necessity? Where are the lines to delineate the permissible and the forbidden, sentimentalism and cold rationalism that can justify any action? I don't know. These questions help me be reconciled with myself, but I can neither forget nor overcome my profound sense of guilt.

When Makhul came to spend the evening with us, it was the first time I'd asked myself why we kept chasing this poor creature and throwing stones at him, as though he were a dog, cat, bird, or squirrel. When I arrived in America, the first thing I noticed was the positive relationship between people and squirrels; even American squirrels were different from ours. From childhood I can recall that squirrels were wary of people; they stayed away and lived in high places like tall oak trees and thick walnut trees. When Makhul paid us a visit on that cold, rainy night, I was shocked; actually I was afraid he had come to complain to my father. I've never forgotten the beating my father gave me when I stole a bunch of green onions from the "Morning Star" garden owned by Farah Rumiya. I didn't usually bring home stolen goods; I was well aware what would happen if I did. But that time I thought things would be different because I was expecting mujadara for dinner, and it's a sin to eat mujadara without green onions. Even so I got a severe beating and was sent to bed without any dinner.

I decided to confront the issue head on, so I sat by the fire next to Makhul. He never even mentioned that we used to chase him, and that made me feel even more guilty. I tried to pay special attention to him; it occurred to me that, of all the village boys, I was actually the one who showed the least enthusiasm for chasing and torturing him. I was surprised to see my father show him such respect. He offered him a glass of arak and peeled him some dawwam (the fruit of the oak tree, in those days just like village chestnuts) that we roasted over the fire. I clearly recall that, when my father started singing some ataba, Makhul wept silently. My father carried on singing, and Makhul cried. I have kept within me the image of Makhul's tears falling, clinging to his mustache and short beard, reflecting both the fire that flickered inside the stove and the other fire that burned within him beneath the thick ashes of his life. From that moment on, I realized that my father had a wonderful voice. Otherwise how could it have penetrated Makhul's skin and bones, working deep inside him and prompting such buried feelings? Now I was also convinced that Makhul himself was not devoid of feelings. He must have had to keep thousands of desires, torments, and daily insults repressed inside him and to bury them deep under mounds of oblivion, all in an ongoing attempt to adjust to his own reality. Suddenly suppression comes to an end, and the dams of forgetfulness collapse. (What psychiatrist can replicate what ataba manages to do?) His feelings pour forth like a spring bursting from the depths of the earth. At that precise moment I came to understand why we call small springs "eyes" of water.

I felt guilty then and I still do. I resolved that, from then on, anyone who harassed Makhul would find me standing alongside him ready to pursue his harassers. I put my slingshot (my best weapon at the time) at his disposal. But Makhul did not live long. Afterward I replaced my slingshot with words—they being, then as now, the only weapon I have truly mastered.

"Do you remember the incident involving Askess," I asked my beloved, "that black American who killed seven policemen before they killed him?"

"Yes, I remember," she replied, clearly surprised by the abrupt change in my free associations, "but what's the connection with Makhul?"

"An obvious one, I think. Their situations were the same: both were abandoned, harassed, and threatened when they were fully grown men. But whereas Askess decided to rebel, Makhul just cried. I made him a slingshot of his own, but he wouldn't take it."

"But the way Askess attacked the police and killed seven of them is outrageous."

"You mention Askess as an attacker, but you don't talk about self-defense. American movies always show Native Americans ambushing and attacking innocent families, usually including an old man, a beautiful woman, and a child. Israel calls its army the 'defense force.' It's occupied the West Bank, the Golan Heights, and the Gaza Strip, and yet it's still a 'defense force.' It's reached as far as Beirut, but it's still a 'defense force.' It's demolished homes on top of families and yet has remained defensive."

"But the way Askess killed seven policemen is violence taken to absurd lengths."

"True enough, but I still agree with his mother's claim that the police harassed him on some trifling pretexts. Once he realized that what they really had in mind was to kill his manhood and pride, he refused to give in. He kept running away from them until he found himself forced to confront them. Then he killed seven of them before he was hit by a hail of bullets."

"Now I remember the incident clearly. At the time I think President Nixon declared Askess's criminal acts to be a violation of law and order."

"That's right. But how can the hero of Watergate claim the right to talk about law and order? What an enormous capacity for hypocrisy, expressed so politely and elegantly! Suave and humble, he appealed to God and Jesus and called on people to pray for peace on Christmas Eve. Then he sent airplanes to bomb hospitals and schools in Vietnam. All he had to do was issue an order, and all the pilots had to do was press a button so the missiles would fire. They all got medals to decorate their broad chests. This is killing of a new order: you just press a button and never have to face your victims. Nixon's elegant suits and pilots were never bloodstained. As for you, you vile pilot who dropped the nuclear bomb on Hiroshima, I was really upset when you said recently that you don't feel any guilt about it and that you would commit the very same crime again if your government asked you."

"I can't forget the sight of that young Vietnamese woman: her house, the one in which she was born, completely destroyed, and her husband and young child killed. With no warning, everything she owned had vanished in the blink of an eye. She wept as she walked in a daze over the smoking ruins of her own home; as she did so, she looked utterly lost and crazy with anguish."

"That scene's exactly like another one that happened in this country. A young American woman, whose husband had been killed in Vietnam, was asked by a television reporter how she felt. 'I can never forgive this country,' she answered angrily. 'It sent the best of our youth to die in faraway lands. What business is it of ours? Before my husband died, he wrote me a letter. He said he had no respect for the rulers of South Vietnam; he felt he was defending thieves and fighting against freedom fighters and idealists. I've been studying history since childhood, and before now I'd formed a clear opinion about our system. But that image has been shattered, and I've no desire to pick up the scattered pieces.'

"When her husband was killed, she came to see the truth, just as Paul did on the road to Damascus. She's no longer willing to justify murder."

"The worst justification I've ever heard came from an American official who explained that dropping a nuclear bomb on Hiroshima was actually a 'humane act' because it ended the war. Even worse was the statement of the pilot who dropped the bomb and of Admiral Zumwalt who was commander of American naval forces in Vietnam. You remember, his daughter was my student; she was actually very nice. He's the one who gave the order for forests to be sprayed with Agent Orange. It's ironic that his own son was fighting on land, underneath that deadly fog. Now the son has cancer, and, as a direct consequence of exposure to that chemical, his grandson was born mentally retarded. The admiral admits that, at least indirectly, he's responsible. Even so, he insists that he doesn't feel guilty and says he'd be prepared to issue the same order today, if needed. Obedience to the state has been turned into a moral code."

My beloved was anxious to change the subject, and I realized she was right. Amid such a gorgeous symphony of colors why, I wondered, did we keep being harried by gloomy images. Even so, I still found myself commenting, "The same story gets repeated: Reagan replaced Nixon. They gave Israel the green light to invade Lebanon."

"That other ass, what's his name? This Secretary of State? Alexander . . . Alexander Haig?"

"And the one after him—who'll remember George Shultz in the future? Whenever I see him on television, he seems to have so much hatred inside him that it wouldn't surprise me if he grew horns on the spot."

"And then there's that perpetual smiler who kept using the language of medieval times to categorize the entire world as either barbaric or civilized societies . . . ."

"And all in order to justify killing."

I can't change the subject either. These gloomy images show no mercy. All I'm looking for is forgiveness, reconciliation, and the enjoyment of love, beauty, and art. Apologetically I continue the conversation, "America's relationship with the rest of the world is like 'El Niño,' which causes floods and droughts. Where rain isn't needed, it manages to pour down in torrents and sweep away everything in its path. But where it is needed, it disappears and the land is left to crack open from drought."

"The word in Spanish actually means 'little boy.' I've no idea why they've given it such a name."

"Nor do I."

Silently we continue our walk along winding footpaths, hoping our harried feelings will go away and leave us alone.

# The Assassination of Wildflowers

I recall a trip to southern Lebanon on a beautiful spring day. We were enchanted by fields of wildflowers, stretching away into the distance as far as the eye could see. It was during those same spring days that Israel invaded those fields, and so I went back to the photographs we had taken. I imagined the tanks of the Israeli defense force trampling over the wildflowers. George, I hope your family was not in any danger. And you, Hasan, where are you? How are things, I wonder, with Adaysa and the spring we drank from till we had quenched our thirst?

So, Mike Anderson, my neighbor, let me ask you: who's the defender and who's the aggressor? Who's the murderer, and who's the victim? Who's civilized, and who's barbaric? Who's the hero, and who's the coward? Your government wants to wipe Cuba, Nicaragua, Iran, Lebanon, and Syria off the face of the earth. And still you're proud of having killed a large number of Japanese (whom you call "Japs") during the Second World War. Why do you harbor so much hatred inside yourself? What motivates you to get up early every morning and raise the American flag in front of your house? My questions are in vain. What can voiceless peoples, the weak, actually do? I want you to know that I stand with Makhul who did not resist. Some weak people resist when they feel their dignity is threatened. From their death they will fashion their history. Don't forget that we celebrate the rites of death, not of birth. To describe us you can use any adjective you like, but heroes are always convinced they're heroes. For heroes, what matters is retaining their integrity. Don't forget that history is struggle. Your weapon consists of classifying heroes as terrorists and traitors as moderates; your government defines moderates as people who want to establish a friendly relationship with America and serve its interests. That's the only way it looks at things. Do oppressed people have interests? When you think you're making fools of the world and history, you're actually fooling yourselves. How can you justify crushing wildflowers? I'll just repeat what Lincoln told you: there's no escaping history; it records those who follow the path of goodness and those who prefer the path of evil.

The vast majority of people in our village consisted of poor families, people who had to sweat long and hard to eat their little portion of bread. No money, no education, no opportunity. Yes, Mr. Anderson, we were backward. Even so, the village had two or three notable families who maintained a strong relationship with the feudal lords of the area and with the political, religious, and business elite. When these important officials visited our village during elections or festivals, the notable families in our village competed and sometimes even fought amongst themselves to be their hosts; in the eyes of lesser families, this made them seem even more influential and gave them still further control over the rest of the village. They used to hit each other with rods and stones—no exaggeration. It would be a furious struggle, just like the fights the weak folk would launch against each other whenever there was disagreement about priority in changing the course of the stream that irrigated their fields. I still recall an unforgettable scene: a man with his head cut open, blood pouring down his face, neck, and clothes.

One day the son of a notable family in our village grabbed a ball that my father had bought me on one of his trips and ran home with it. I burst into tears and returned defeated to my own home. Apparently my father had been watching the scene from the roof. He came downstairs and was waiting for me at the crossroads. It was only when we were face-to-face that I even noticed him. With no further inquiry or explanation, he told me to go back and get the ball, whatever the consequences. He warned me not to come home without it. His determination left no room for hesitation. Without tears I retraced my tracks, well aware that our neighbor was stronger than me; so far no one had dared challenge him. But now confrontation was inevitable. I entered the fray and was surprised to discover that the notable family's son wasn't as strong as I thought he'd be. I threw him on the ground, yanked the ball out of his hand, and walked proudly home. My father was still waiting. He didn't say a word, but put his arm around my shoulder; we walked home together. Once there, he cracked a walnut, wrapped it in a piece of malban, and offered it to me. Mr. Anderson, you've no idea what it means to eat walnuts with malban. My Aunt Nazira still sends me malban in America, and my Aunt Fahida sends me supplies of shanklish, as does my Aunt Latifa. I'll tell you frankly that, when Azmi 'Abd al-Qadir gets his house in Jerusalem back, I've promised to offer him walnuts and malban.

There is something else I want to tell you, Mr. Anderson. While hiking in the Shenandoah Mountains, I listened to a tape given to me by Hanna, the cantor in the Orthodox Church in Washington. Do you want to know what's on the tape? It is a Qur'an recitation by Shaykh Mustafa Ismail. As we were climbing in the Shenandoah Mountains, his voice rose, calm and dignified, chanting the Sura of the Ant:

*We gave knowledge to David and Solomon . . .*
*He [Solomon] said: "O ye people! We have been taught the speech of birds . . . ."*
*And before Solomon were marshaled his hosts of jinns and men and birds . . . .*
*At length, when they came to a valley of ants, one of the ants said:*
*"O ye ants, get into your habitations,*
*lest Solomon and his hosts crush you underfoot without knowing . . . ."*
*She said: "Kings, when they enter a country, despoil it;*
*they transform the noblest of its people into its meanest . . . ."*
*"Go back to them, and be sure that when we return,*
*we bring enough hordes to expel them from there in disgrace,*
*and they will feel humbled (indeed)."*

These are symbols, Mr. Anderson. Yesterday I read that a Zionist concluded that, in the hands of an Arab, the Qur'an was a bomb, so he shot him. My own listening to the Qur'an is symbolic. If I'd been looking for entertainment, I would have listened to Frank Sinatra who sings for dejected soldiers as they languish in heavily guarded military bases. Why do I mention such insignificant names? I don't know. I shouldn't. Maybe it's because you like them, you who'd like his government to wipe rebellious societies off the face of the earth and who feels proud for killing a number of Japanese.

I apologize, Mr. Anderson. I've been very frank in expressing my feelings to you, but I don't want you to conclude that I hate you. You'd be wrong to think that. I really empathize with you. I want to congratulate you on your wife's successful surgery. All I wanted to do was to warn you not to grab the ball and assassinate the flowers. I realize you'll never be able to distinguish between murderer and victim. If you like, you can give me a lecture on democracy; I've no objection. I can listen now just as I've done so often in the past. But I want you to realize that I'm over fifty years old and I've never voted, not even once. That's my sole comment on democracy. I'm like Bob Frost, who never registered or voted; he preferred playing the flute rather than deceiving himself into thinking that he had any real choice in the matter.

I am backward, from a Third World country. You may have noticed that, whenever I get out of my car, I give the rear end a pat, though I'm sure you don't know why. When I was a child, I used to ride a mule; when I dismounted, I'd pat his rear thankfully. It's just a habit from the distant past. We even treat cars like living creatures and thank them. A few days ago my mother asked me if my brother had currycombed the mule; what she meant to ask was whether he'd washed the car. I can understand why you're surprised that I'm a professor at one of America's finest universities. Yesterday I read that some young white American men had attacked Cambodian immigrants because, within three years of their arrival in America, the Cambodians had managed to achieve what they themselves had failed to achieve during their entire life. That sort of aggression would never have happened if it weren't for the general atmosphere created by the policies of your highly esteemed government. I can assure you that I'm not unaware of the contradictions and conflicting trends that exist in the West. Yesterday, I read a poem by a university student. Here's an excerpt:

*I am a Westerner.*
*I was a guest of a Sudanese family in Khartoum,*
*Where the White Nile meets the Blue Nile.*
*There is no rain in Sudan.*
*There is hunger in Sudan.*
*There are people and sunshine in Sudan.*
*I eat all day long.*

*I eat cheese, falafil, liver, salad, and dates.*
*I drink tea.*
*I am a guest in Sudan.*
*I am a Westerner.*
*We ride in air-conditioned Mercedes cars.*
*But I cannot distinguish*
*Between the White Nile and the Blue Nile.*

The university student's name is Isabel. Would you like to meet her, Mr. Anderson? I don't know what you'd think of her. Most likely, you'd denounce her as a communist. That way you can save yourself the bother of searching for the truth.

# Another Generation of Forests

From my imaginary voyages I returned to reality. "Congratulations, Don Quixote," I told myself, "on your illusory victories!" My wife was collecting leaf samples. I asked her whether she'd marry me again if we got divorced. She didn't hesitate. In the past she'd often repeated her mistakes, she said, but this was one mistake she wasn't going to repeat. "I wouldn't agree to a divorce anyway," I told her, "because I'd have to ask for your hand all over again."

I gave her a hug, then let her go. Side by side we walked down narrow back paths and then returned to the main track. We were reading a small sign about a kind of tree and its relationship to life and death, when suddenly a chipmunk jumped in front of us and vanished inside the trunk. The sign informed us that, "A dead tree is very much alive. When it dies, it can no longer resist infestation by beetles, bacteria, and fungi. As the wood softens, ants, centipedes, grubs, and worms move in. A rotting tree is very like an apartment house; it provides homes for many living creatures. With time it disintegrates and returns to the soil, nourishment for yet another generation of trees."

These words penetrated to my inner core, and there they multiplied. I thought about the forests of the future, born from the roots of other murdered forests. Nothing endures, but nothing ends either. Death is not a journey to some other world. Is that how you see things, Elias al-Akhras?

My face is shrouded in sorrow, its shadows reflected in my beloved's eyes. I think of lakes as mirrors of sky and trees, and address the crane once more. "After each death," I ask, "will my departure and rebirth be like yours?"

All this was at harvest time, the end of spring and beginning of summer. The golden stalks of wheat swayed back and forth in harmony with the rolling hills, meeting and touching like ballet dancers in *Swan Lake* or *The Nutcracker*.

As hot day turned into rainy night, trees, roads, and houses were rinsed of their dust and bathed in cool breezes. My father had washed off the day's weariness and climbed into the hammock he'd put up between two trees in front of our house so he could sleep there during the summer. Najib and Mighal came over and spent a long time telling him about a dispute they'd had that day over who should be allowed to irrigate his land first.

I fell asleep before they'd finished. By the time I woke up next morning, my father wasn't there. My mother told me that he'd gone off to Marmarita with the dentist on some job or other. He'd spend a day or two there, then go on to Habb Nimra to get a new saddle for his mule.

Two days later he came home, looking sick and bent double with pain. That night, his condition worsened, and he couldn't sleep. My mother called my grandfather Salim and my uncles Jamil and Yusuf. When our neighbors heard about it, they came over as well to spend the night with my father. Before dawn they sent my uncle Jamil to al-Mashta to fetch Dr. Tu'ma. I can't remember where I was exactly; I suppose I must have been asleep. According to my mother, my uncle came back an hour later and told them the doctor had refused to come without payment of three lira in advance. She gave him the money, and he returned to al-Mashta. All of a sudden my father began to feel better. He got up, washed his face, and talked about various things with my grandfather and Uncle Yusuf.

When the doctor arrived, he examined my father carefully and joked around with him. He decided my father had pneumonia, so he gave him an injection. He gave my mother instructions about his care, and then left to pay a visit to a notable family next door. The visitors left too, and my father went back to bed. My mother meanwhile went to prepare the compress the doctor had ordered, and I stayed with him on my own. That's all I can remember, but my mother told me he lost consciousness as soon as the doctor gave him that cursed injection. Thereafter she would count up the doctor's other victims from our village and the surrounding district.

I can remember that my father motioned to me to sit next to him. I approached him tentatively, just as I had with the injured crane. I saw his face, bronzed the color of honey, grow ever paler. Outside, clouds returned to encircle the earth and smother its breath; their dark shadows entered the house and lingered where I sat beside my father. The air was still and weighed heavily on his chest—thick, rainless clouds. I sat by him, alone, while my mother lit the fire outside and prepared the compress. He didn't say anything to me, nor could I think of what to say to him. I didn't know how to bandage his broken wing.

He stretches his hand out to grasp mine; it is hot and trembling. He tries to smile, but his expression is cold, pale, and gaunt; no longer his usual smile. Terrified, I drown in that deep silence, having no idea what to say. Dark shadows from the clouds lurk on the walls and almost shroud the corners in darkness. I recall that the house had been this dark during the silk-culling seasons the year before. My mother had rented some mulberry trees to raise silkworms. In order to fund the project she had borrowed money, hoping to pay it back at the end of the season, and had sold her sewing machine as well. It had turned out to be a very bad season that year; in fact Abbud al-Haddad had immortalized what happened in some zajal songs, one verse of which talked about my mother:

*Maryam raised silkworms*
*Only one cocoon survived*
*A whistle she bought with it*
*to pacify little Halim.*

At such times village people can be quite extraordinary; they keep their sanity by making light of misfortunes, then behaving as if nothing had happened. And yet, even if this legacy was part of my upbringing and is now an integral element in my temperament, I admit that I can still get very emotional. I feel deeply sorry for you, Abbud al-Haddad. You hoped to die with dignity, but instead you lived long and suffered much. You went to stay with your children in Beirut so the village wouldn't have to witness your last affliction. In your glory days the village was your stage: no one could equal you at the dabka or singing, and you entranced young women when you danced at weddings and festivals.

I'd like to tell you that Maryam, the one who rented mulberry trees to raise silk and failed in her first commercial venture, had a hard struggle after my father's death. She gathered the harvest in the eastern plains, baked for people in the village, worked as a maid in Beirut, washed clothes, swept and mopped floors, ironed, and cooked—all so she could send us to the best schools and preserve our sense of dignity. She devoted herself to the task, working tirelessly. Whenever she was on her own, I'd hear her reciting zajal verses to herself:

*Unavoidable are misery and hardship.*
*Plenty will come; anxious days will pass.*
*The long branch will bend,*
*The short branch will grow.*
*Lovers must part*
*Even when bound by the strongest twine.*

No doubt you too used to recite poems about patience and hope; you can surely recall the line that goes, "Be patient, oh heart, so the burden may ease." But struggle and pride have to be there too. For me, as a poor child among rich pupils at school, such pride was never an issue. Because of my mother's job I never felt at ease with rich people; I always felt that my relationships with them were based on humiliation, particularly when couched in the form of pity. I hate the word "pity" just as much as I love the word "justice." That has had a major impact on my attitude toward religion. Don't ask me how; I don't know. I used to feel such things very deeply. My relationships with rich children were tense, especially when I beat them all at school. They'd retaliate with nasty taunts, such as "Poor folk are only poor because they're lazy." One of the ladies my mother worked for suggested that I quit school so that I could work and help with the family upkeep, but my mother ignored her advice. She was too modest to ask, "Who'd teach your children if my son left school?"

Oh, now I've remembered what I wanted to tell you. My mother's old now, no longer the person you or I used to know. I'll tell you a secret I've never told anyone before, something I don't think I've even dared admit to myself. You and I know, in fact everyone knows, just how much my mother did for us, how she deprived herself for our sake. I am doing my best to pay her back for all her travails, to give her a life of dignity and happiness in her latter days. There were problems even before she had her fall. For some time her life had become full of illusions and doubts, and yet she never gave a thought to herself. However, once she turned eighty-seven, she withdrew into herself and could only focus on her own problems. What scares her most now is the idea of not being able to look after herself any more. "Oh God," she says over and over again, "Once I fall, please take me to my grave." Then came that bad fall, but the grave refused to claim her. Now she's buried above ground, not beneath. Even before she fell, she wasn't happy about her relationships with other people. She'd pray constantly to God, begging Him to take pity on her, to help her bear her pain, to soften people's hearts toward her, and to protect her from her enemies. To overcome the fear, loneliness, and sheer tedium she felt, she transformed her life into a set of rituals centered around her own problems and illusions. She had already become very forgetful about names, faces, facts, things she'd said or heard. After her fall, she forgot everything. It's really hard to watch your own mother declining so completely.

She won't let me help her. Deeply ingrained in her psyche is the notion that children should listen to their parents, not the other way round. When she ignored my advice, I'd really lose my temper with her. Needless to say, I tried to be patient, knowing full well that I ought to overlook her continual slip-ups. But you can't always keep your self-control. I'd get angry, shout, swear, and threaten, all in vain. She never realized she was wrong. On the very rare occasions she did realize and admitted it, she'd totally disarm me. "Let God take me now," she'd say, "I've gone senile. Please be patient with me, son, and forgive me." Sometimes she'd try to make me feel guilty (she was very good at that) by reminding me of all the sacrifices she'd made; that would make me more furious than ever. With time I began to counter these tactics with a withering sarcasm. "My father didn't die," I'd tell her, "he ran away." That used to get her riled, but eventually she learned to put up with that too. The most important lesson I've learned from it all is that a person must learn when to die; I only hope I'll know when it's time to resign from life. There can be nothing in life more wretched than being totally preoccupied with oneself. I feel the utmost pity for people who are so busy with themselves and their own personal salvation that they can't make any contribution to saving the world. This may be why Americans are so unhappy and feel a loneliness as deep as the depths of the desert.

This is what happened to my mother even before she had her fall. Afterward her problems simply became more complicated and profound, taking on totally new forms. Now talking to her has become an ordeal; she no longer understands me. Maybe I don't understand myself. What a mercy it would be if death came before it's too late! Yet how difficult death is in the flower of youth. That reminds me of Elias al-Akhras. He married late and had a son who brought him much happiness. His son grew up and, like Adonis, he went out hunting. He never came back. They found his body later. Had he been gored by a wild boar, just like Adonis? However, his blood never flowed into the river, and from that day spring-water never flowed into the life of Elias al-Akhras either. Oh Elias, death in youth is as hard as granite. Now you too are surely dead and at rest.

My father's hand reaches out to take mine. He puts it to his lips and kisses it. He draws me toward him and lays his face against mine, laughing as he feels me try to wriggle my own face away. "Am I scratching you?" he asks. "I haven't shaved today."

Suddenly his hands rise toward the ceiling, then come down again slowly. He grinds his teeth, and I stare at him terrified. In his eyes I see a total change; no doubt, he is staring death in the face. Unable to move, I yell for my mother in a strangled voice. He was still gnashing his teeth.

# Profound Sorrow and Happiness

I wake up abruptly from a nightmare. Beneath a huge tree in the Shenandoah Mountains I can feel my beloved's hand on my shoulder, perching like a tiny bird on my branches. A golden leaf trembles, falls into a brook in Kafrun, and is quickly swept toward the falls.

"Do you remember," I ask my beloved, "Makhada Falls in Kafrun?"

"You call those falls?" she replied. "You can't compare them with even the smallest falls on the Potomac. What's made you think of them now?"

"The crane."

"The crane?"

"Yes. The crane's made me think of them. It reminds me of the child who asked his mother where he came from. 'The stork brought you,' she told him. 'So where did our neighbor's children come from?' he asked next. 'Samir came out of a head of cabbage,' she replied, 'Fadi came out of a head of lettuce, Fadya came out of a rose, and Salim came out of an apple.' At this point the child interrupted. 'Don't men and women sleep together in this town?' he asked."

My beloved didn't laugh, even to humor me. We'd both heard

the joke so many times, it wasn't funny any more. "You still haven't told me," she repeated, "why the crane made you think of Makhada Falls."

"It carried them in that hard, long beak, under its huge wings."

"Don't be daft!"

I realize she meant what she said. Her expression grew yet more morose as she waited for me to give a serious answer.

"When you put your hand on my shoulder," I said quietly, "I was daydreaming. At first I thought it was a bird perching on a sycamore branch by the riverbank in Kafrun. When it hopped on to another branch, a leaf fell into the river, and the current swept it away to a small waterfall."

The current of death had snatched my father away to another world, his face faded like a golden leaf in autumn. Death came down to Kafrun that overlooks its green valleys below and searched out my father's weary soul. He'd suffered long in fruitless vineyards. Now death arrived, swooping down like an eagle, snatched him away and flew far off. .

Tears were shed, by the broken-hearted wife and the son. The lonely, desolate daughter wept and wept. The handsome small one who'd inherited his father's features didn't understand what was happening, yet he too sensed that a tragedy had entered his world. They all saw death approach, swooping to earth like an eagle and plucking my father from his homeland with no chance to whisper a farewell. Sadly the little one knew nothing of that other abode. My mother appealed for help, and neighbors and relatives came rushing over. The church bells tolled in sorrow. "Who's died?" asked little Fahida.

"Your brother, you poor thing!" they told her. She lowered the bundle of corn from her head, took off her wooden clogs, and ran off barefoot. Next moment, the face of Marianna, so compassionate, beautiful, loving, and cheerful, was transformed as her habitual smile was replaced by terror, and she too ran off barefoot and weeping to the house of her favorite cousin. All the other villagers arrived, then more people from nearby villages. They called the doctor, who was still on his visit to the village notable. He sipped the rest of his coffee, then came over reluctantly. The visitors cleared a way to the bed. He looked at my father, briefly checked his pulse, and pronounced him dead. He consoled my mother with a pat on the shoulder, intoning "God compensate your loss with many years of life," leaned down to kiss me, then darted out.

I felt completely lost in the crowd of people who were all weeping and wailing. I'd heard of death before, seen it face to face even, but till this moment I had never felt it with such bitterness. I plunged into a well of tears and hid, but people kept hugging me, so my cries were mingled with theirs. When I heard them weeping, I sighed; when they heard me sighing, they filled the skies with their lamentations. To this very day I can still see my mother beating her face and breast with her hands. When I started beating my own face, she clasped me to her breast and wept more softly. Our neighbor whispered to Ghassan to take me to their house. He came over, along with Jamal, Nasri, and Salim, and they wrenched me away. They washed my face in cold water and brought mankala, then persuaded me to play with them to cheer me up. I surprised myself by going along with the idea.

"Just imagine, I played mankala while my father lay dead."

In telling my beloved that detail, yet another long-buried secret was revealed. I'd never dared tell anyone before; whenever it had come to mind, I'd tried to keep it buried by busying myself with other things.

"Why are you thinking about all these things now?" my beloved protested. "How strange you are! Why can't you enjoy this magical world? Could there be anything more delightful?"

"Believe me, I am enjoying it. I'm not sad. As far as I can see, there must be some thin, invisible thread linking utter grief to total happiness. Once in a while, I get the feeling that, for children in our village, death was a type of fun, one of our most unusual games. I've already told you that we used to make our own toys. We couldn't afford to buy them readymade like city children. When they get bored with one toy, all they can do is buy another one. Toys become just like their own lives: they start piling up in forgotten corners—they're spoiled rotten. Whenever someone in the village died, we children would drop everything and go off to the cemetery. We'd watch the expressions on people's faces, listen to hymns, climb trees, or else peer through people's legs at the casket as it was lowered into the grave and showered with earth and rocks. After the mourners had left, we'd pick acorns and gallnuts from the huge oak trees. Acorns were our chestnuts, and we'd use gallnuts to play games or make bets."

"Whenever we encounter death," she replied, "I realize that we get extremely emotional, exactly the opposite of western people. With them it's all elaborate solemnity, whereas we go overboard on weeping. It's never occurred to me before that death could be a game."

Then I remembered the terrible occasion when my beloved had seen the bodies of her father, her brother and his wife, and her aunt, in a funeral home in Detroit. Her tears had turned into breathless sobs, and she had almost fainted in my arms. I had yelled at her to control herself, but her uncle, the physician, pushed me aside and told people to give her room to breathe.

Confronted with such memories, I decided to change the subject. "I didn't believe autumn could be so beautiful," I said, leaping up to reach for a low branch glowing with colors, "even more so than spring. These colors are a kind of enchanting symphony; their harmony is like glorious music."

I'll never forget the evening we heard Beethoven's Ninth Symphony in the Hill Auditorium at the University of Michigan.

Surely that work is the greatest symphony ever produced by the human spirit. I remember the chorus being all round us, and how their voices seemed to move us back and forth, like small boats being tossed by the waves. How sublime to ascend to the heights of the universe, to descend to the depths of the earth! We look down on the Himalayan peaks, we sink to the abyss of Dante's inferno. Oh you waves, storms, thunderbolts, and lightning, shake the world's very foundations, then rebuild it! That's just how I felt today as I faced the waterfalls. Was it that, I wonder, that made me climb down the cliff and cross the tree-bridge to reach a rock in the midst of the rushing river?

I gazed at my beloved. "Ever since I met you," I told her, "the face of my world has been different."

"So has mine," she said.

"I fell into your falls, and your clouds lifted me up."

"You're good with words. That's all you give me."

"They're free, a gift."

"I'll pay you for them if you like."

"They're priceless."

We paused by another plaque describing the history of a crumbled rock with plants growing from its crevices. I remembered the great rock that had given birth to a fig tree in Kafrun and sadly recalled how they'd removed it to make a wide, straight road. I curse those agents of modern culture known as "developers." For them wanton destruction of the environment is progress. Munif, how dare you accuse me of wanting the village to remain backward, just because I spoke out against a project that would dump sewage into the river!

According to that small plaque in the Shenandoah Mountains, the crumbling rocks "are fighting a losing battle against the forces of nature. Lichens, small scale-like plants growing on the rocks, secrete an acid that carves tiny holes in the rocks. Freezing water helps crack and break the rocks, and soil particles collect in the cracks. Small plants start growing in these patches of soil; their roots push into the cracks, forcing the rocks to split. With yet more rain, soil, plants, and roots, more and more cracks appear. These rocks will gradually disappear."

"Death's a case of transformation," I commented.

"True enough."

"Trees and rocks tell us that."

While we were playing mankala, Munif's and Salim's mothers passed by on their way to our house to express their condolences. Seeing me playing, Munif's mother looked at me in astonishment. "Isn't he the deceased's son?" she asked Salim's mother. "The poor little boy's playing. He doesn't know what death means."

"He's only a child," Salim's mother answered. "Poor thing."

Bowing my head in shame and embarrassment, I charged back to our house, only to get lost all over again in the crowd of mourners. They had placed my father in a wooden casket and made the necessary arrangements to take him to the cemetery. Out of pity and concern for my mother and us children they had decided to bury him that very day, just a few hours after his death. His friends carried him to the cemetery where he would lie forever beneath the massive oak trees.

However, this speedy burial did nothing to ease my mother's grief. Quite the contrary, her sorrow grew deeper; indeed it has stayed with her to this very day and will accompany her to the end of her long life. "They took you away from me, my beloved," she kept yelling on the day he died, as the rest of the women restrained her. "They took you away. Give him back to me. His body's still warm. Have you buried him when his body is still warm?" Then she started to sing to him, quietly, "You vanished beneath the earth like a grain of wheat," and "Who will give me springs of tears to weep with?"

The day after my father's burial, a rumor started spreading

that a man from the neighboring village of al-Mahayri walking through the cemetery the previous evening had heard moans from my father's grave and fled in terror. When a neighbor told my mother about the rumor, she fainted. From then on, I tried to invoke whatever scientific principles I had in my grasp to convince her that the rumor couldn't possibly be true. It was all in vain. She is still convinced my father died from the doctor's injection, and the people who buried him just a few hours afterward were barbarians.

Just a few days before she fell down, I was talking to her about times past. She was still angry and bitter. "Above all else," she said, "I'm still bitterly sorry about your father. God take Dr Tu'ma's life! If he hadn't given your father that injection, he would never have died. He'd got out of bed, washed his face, and was talking to us as though nothing was wrong with him. He had talked to his father and his cousin, Yusuf, about his trip to al-Mishtaya, Marmarita, and Habb Nimra. When the doctor gave him that injection, he lost consciousness. That doctor's killed scores of patients—God thwart him! The people in our village are monsters, my son. They buried him while his body was still warm. Why did his father, brothers, and cousins let them do it? They snatched him from me. He died at noon, and they made his casket, dug his grave, and buried him in the afternoon. Why couldn't they leave the burial till next day? That man from al-Mahayri heard him moaning, but instead of rousing the village people, he just ran away. How can you even want me to go back to that village? I can't, I just can't. God blight the lot of them, beasts!"

My mother hates the village just as much as I love it. I've tried in vain to change her mind, but once an idea is stuck in her mind, there is no way of changing it. And for all her deep faith, she has never forgotten how the doctor and the priest took the eight liras my father had left and divided it between them. "Doctors and priests," she'll say, "all they do is grab money from orphans and widows." I have to confess that these words of my mother's, words that I've heard throughout my life, have influenced my own attitudes toward the clergy and the rich.

When I was a student at university, I met a beautiful young woman who, as it turned out, was related in some way to the infamous doctor who had treated my father. We became close friends; in fact, we might well have started a relationship if I hadn't made the mistake one day of telling her the story of the doctor's injection that had, as far as we were concerned, killed my father. She got scared and vanished from my life.

As for the priest who buried my father, I gather he lost his mind later on. In his latter days he'd tear his clothes off and run into streams; at night he'd roam through the vineyards, and his family would have to go out searching for him. People also said he'd go off to the cemetery and collect skulls of the dead, then preach sermons at them, threatening them all with the hellfire. He'd arrange the skulls in a long line, then climb an oak tree and look down to make sure the line was straight. I felt really sorry for him. I was always training myself to rise above petty things and only fight major battles. I plunged wholeheartedly into the world and exposed myself to its various currents. The more I was exposed to life, the greater did my appetite for it become. I engaged the world, fought it, plunged in and traversed its seas; I came to regard my disengagement from it as a kind of asphyxiation, a surefire internal death, like a fish out of water.

Yes, I'm full of suppressed anger. What annoys me most is oppression. When I realize that the history of humanity is a long record of oppression and cruelty, it makes me feel guilty because I haven't devoted my own life to the fight. There's so much killing in the world, so many masks, so much fear. How badly we need to fight alongside Makhul! What am I doing in

Washington and the Shenandoah Mountains? Why wasn't I there in Beirut, when the 1982 siege was on? Why didn't I stand up to the Israeli tanks as they crushed the wildflowers of southern Lebanon? Resistance is the salt of the earth.

So, you civilization of masks, I reject you. I proclaim you despicable and mean. You call freedom-fighters terrorists. You divide the world into two, civilized and barbarous. I declare you barbarians; it's a word I hate, but maybe you can understand your own language. Your elegance is merely a mask. I see a connection between your preoccupation with losing weight and hunger in Africa. Your democracy is a polite, clinical form of rape; and it smells. This very day I read that a rich man saw an advertisement stating that "a Rolls Royce is for those unusual people with an inner motivation to achieve life's loftiest aspirations," and decided on the spot to buy his wife one for her birthday. It costs a hundred and fifty-six thousand dollars, which is more than many poor Third World families have to live on for their entire lives. Oh yes, I know what you'll say: It's his money; he can do what he likes with it. To which I reply that he must be a thief. You jewel thieves of hungry Africa, where will you run to? You women wearing the fur of rare seals clubbed to death in their infancy, where will you flee? You people who smoke cigarettes in holders made from cranes' legs, how long will your tyranny last? When will the limits of exploitation and injustice be reached? When will we put an end to oppression and affluence at the expense of the deprived? You have turned "the other" into a machine as well. Now you've reached the stage of hiring women to have your children. You make a contract with them when they're in desperate straits and insert your sperm into their womb. No sooner has the woman given birth than you snatch the newborn baby from her lap. When any of these women becomes attached to the baby (when, to quote my mother, it's become the flower of her heart) and refuses to give it up, you take her to court and bring all your money and influence to bear against motherhood. You rob humanity of motherhood itself. What are the limits of such affluence and greed? Why do I make do with words as my only weapon?

Why, I wonder, am I so full of anger? Why am I pondering issues like these in such an enchanting atmosphere? How can I be rid of my convictions and anxieties, if only for a moment? For just a single second I would love to be free of worries.

How can I find the nerve to be angry in the midst of this vast delight, this enchanting beauty, this utter peace? Why am I haunted by such issues? How can I be so possessed by them even in this glorious place? Why do I summon the oppressed to abandon their silence, when I can relish such joy, beauty, and serenity? Is it because there can be no real joy, beauty, and serenity in life as long as I cannot share it with others? In vain I try to free myself from my concerns. So, my own self, be filled with concerns! O crane, I'm like you, constantly in flight and being born again.

Why, I wonder, should the death of a tree in the Shenandoah Mountains remind me of so many things, my father's death in Kafrun, the murder of wildflowers, the fall of cranes, my homeland's suicide, and my mother's lingering death? Why this escape to childhood? Why analysis? Where's the dividing line between death and confrontation?

Since leaving Kafrun as a child, I've plunged into the world and joined its battles on all fronts. Without something to fight for, I'm like a fish out of water. In battle I'm like the salmon Hani told me about. They swim up rivers and streams against the current till they reach the place where they were born. Once they arrive after their arduous struggle, they lay their eggs and die.

Like you, O crane, I've crossed continents, flown over mountaintops, and followed rivers and seas. I've exposed myself to death, and on each occasion have been reborn. I've plunged through clouds, translucent and dense, and touched the naked sky. I've stood in the rain, battled tempests, and discovered new horizons. I've left my flock, then rejoined it. I've ranged in all four directions and taken root in the earth. And I've come to know profound sorrow and happiness.

# Leaving the Shell

My beloved handed me a leaf that had just fallen from a lofty tree. I looked at its blazing colors and its stem, with translucent veins spreading through all parts of its surface. I gave the leaf back to my beloved.

"Do you remember," I asked, "the story of the deformed boy with elephantiasis? He grew an enormous, long, powerful arm."

"The one who used to beat up all the other kids, you mean, including his brothers and sisters?"

"That's the one. His parents always had to defend him. They asked the other kids to stay away from him and show some understanding because he was sick, sensitive, and had a complex."

"I know exactly. But why are you reminding me of this story?"

I was sure she actually knew, but I wanted to test her. "Why do you think?"

"You see Israel as the boy, and America as the parent that always has to defend it."

"That's it!"

"Here I show you a beautiful, colored leaf that's just fallen from this tree, and all you can talk about is the deformed boy, Israel, and America. That's weird. Get rid of your nightmares."

"You're right again!"

"I don't want to hear any more about that subject for a while."

"I promise."

So I looked at the leaf's blazing colors again, but it was no use. Instead I heard voices approaching from al-Shaqif Castle in southern Lebanon: "Abu Ali to 402. Direct the air in our direction and hold on. Send the birds and say, 'Hold your ground.'"

We are looking down on yet another valley and a hill shrouded in a transparent layer of fog. I feel myself scattered in a variety of directions all at once. A few days before she fell down, my mother unleashed her captive voice, which crackled its way through a calm, sad song:

*Others' fortune tree gave dates and fruits,*
*Mine is but a barren linden tree.*

She falls silent. Slowly her voice rises in song, like fog over the valley, but I can't tell whether it tells of joy or sorrow. I want it to include anger as well:

*North they went, and their horses raced south.*
*They tortured me, O mother, like thread inside a needle.*
*By the tombs of the saints and mountain dwellers,*
*With their departure I lost my will to live.*

Once again she falls silent, searching her confused memory for another verse. At first it doesn't come. "Woe is me!" she says, as though talking to herself rather than me, "I've forgotten everything, and my voice no longer works." But then her voice rises again, an endless blend of joy and sorrow:

*I climbed to the mountain peak,*
*And called my friends.*

*My color yellowed, and I said,*
*"Death has come for me."*
*O writers of letters,*
*Write me of their meanings.*
*Then I shall sit by the roadside,*
*with no one to deliver them.*

I hand her a glass of arak and a bite of shanklish, and she forgets her sorrow. "God keep you!" she says. "Cheers! Just one sip to toast you with. No more!" She settles back in her chair and moves on to another type of song, just as Nasim al-Nab used to do:

*O Dal'una, love of my heart,*
*If you don't want me, just leave me alone.*
*One day Love's breeze will blow westward,*
*Then I'll see to whom you belong.*

Picking up the glass of arak she takes another sip. I hand her a slice of tomato, and she asks if I've sprinkled salt on it, which she loves. She continues singing:

*She came proudly toward me and said: If you please,*
*I am just a young maid, not of your generation*
*I plead with you in the name of God, the secrets of your Gospels,*
*And the seven creeds and whomever you worship. . . .*

We applauded her, well aware of how rarely she now emerged from her melancholy shell. We asked her to sing some more, so she decided to end her recital with a strophe of ataba. She fell silent, cleared her throat, and then was silent again. The words floated up from her chest like tiny birds soaring over valleys:

*I sighed, and I sighed, and I sighed.*
*Like the tireless water wheel I sighed.*
*But for patience and simile, I would have gone mad long ago*
*And sought the companionship of wild beasts.*

Again she falls silent, still cupping her cheek in her hand. We leave her alone in order to talk about serious matters. She is still floundering in her own private world and keeps singing softly, as though to apologize for her continuing urge to sing:

*Ah . . . the sorrows of my life.*
*How the wolf delights when the shepherd departs.*
*Ah . . . Sigh after sigh, but I am never cured.*
*The fire in my heart will never be extinguished.*

I relive all those memories as we make our way down, leaving behind us the enchanting Shenandoah Mountains that will be stripped bare of leaves in just a few days by the advent of winter storms and snow. What will happen to the deer?

At midpoint we stop by a spring, have a drink, and fill up a container that we have brought with us for just such a purpose. It's almost like a reprise of our very first meeting in Aitha al-Fukhar village. A young black woman comes up to have a drink too, and I suggest to her that she use cupped hands, the way we did in Kafrun. I smile as she tries, and she smiles back. She is beautiful and sad too, like morning in Shenandoah autumn. I repeat to myself:

*Descend, O death, descend*
*Descend into Savannah in Georgia*
*Into the depths of Yamakro*
*And search for sister Carolina.*

I go back to my beloved in the car. "You devil," she asks with a smile, "what were you saying to that young black woman?"

"I told her that I was crazy about her."

"You devil."

We make our way back to Washington, listening to a cassette with a short oud solo by Munir Bashir. As we listen, we both sigh, with joy at first, then in sorrow, then both together. Afterward we listen to another tape of the poet, Adonis, reciting a poem like rains falling on Qassabin or fire devouring forest on blazing hot California afternoons.

*Our fire is approaching the city,*
*To destroy the city's bed*
*. . . Our fire is approaching, and grass is born from its*
*seething embers.*
*Our fire is approaching the city.*

We reach the city and pick up our lives as before. We hurry through its streets, tossed by waves of people, sinking and rising to the surface again. The salt of the waves penetrates to our very core.

We plunge into the world as though it were a real battle. We swim against the current and hover over rivers. We traverse the faces—flattened, wrinkled, black, white, intelligent, stupid, defeated, arrogant, full, empty, happy, sad. We free ourselves of melancholy and sing the ode to joy.

Was our return inevitable?

# Glossary

**‘Abd al-Wahhab and Farid al-Atrash:** two of the Arab world’s most famous singers of the twentieth century.

**arak:** the most popular alcoholic drink in the Fertile Crescent, made—like ouzo—from anise.

**ataba:** a popular colloquial poetic genre, sung throughout the villages of the Fertile Crescent.

**dabka:** a traditional folk dance, performed by groups of young men and women.

**dal‘una:** a rhythmic colloquial poetic genre, with a fixed rhyme scheme.

**dawwam:** the nuts of the oak tree.

**ful:** a dish of fava beans mixed with garlic, lemon, and olive oil.

**hummus:** a famous dish made from chickpeas crushed with tahini, garlic, and lemon.

**jinns:** guardian spirits who can be forces for good or evil (from which comes the English word, ‘genie’).

**kibbeh:** a dish prepared with extra-lean ground meat mixed with bulghur.

**kishik:** a traditional Syrian dish made of dried yogurt.

**ma‘anna:** a rhythmic colloquial poetic genre, with a fixed rhyme scheme.

**malban:** a Syrian sweet.

**mankala:** a Syrian board game.

**mezze:** a selection of traditional appetizers, usually served with alcoholic beverages.

**mijana:** a rhythmic colloquial poetic genre, with a fixed rhyme scheme.

**mujadara:** a traditional Syrian dish, made of lentils with either bulghur or rice.

**mutabala:** a dish made of wheat and chickpeas, mixed with yogurt.

**nay:** a Middle Eastern flute.

**oud:** a lute.

**qalalih:** gallnuts, from the oak tree.

**Qamar al-Zaman:** literally 'moon of the ages,' a prominent female figure in an *Arabian Nights* tale.

**al-Salaamu 'alaykum:** the traditional Muslim greeting, 'Peace be upon you.'

**shanklish:** a traditional Syrian dish of aged cheese.

**shubassi:** colloquial Syrian term for watchman.

**sirwal:** loose pants, traditionally worn by men, bound with a sash.

**Sura of the Ant:** the twenty-seventh chapter (sura) of the Qur'an.

**tabouleh:** the Lebanese national dish; a salad made with bulghur wheat, tomatoes, and parsley.

**umm:** mother.

**zajal:** a widespread form of popular poetry, with a fixed rhyme scheme and rhythm.

# Translators' Afterword

In *The Crane*, Halim Barakat gives us a sensitive and honest personal account of his life. In this short autobiographical novel he recalls his past and documents a life-voyage of rootlessness, nostalgia, alienation, and continuous exile, all couched in a poetic style. The reader follows the writer on this headlong journey, seeking answers to the difficult questions that the novel raises. Beyond this, Barakat manages to transcend his own experiences, parlaying them into a more universal statement, one that applies to all Arab intellectuals enduring oppression and banishment. With its critical insights into fifty years of the author's life, the novel offers a frank revelation of the author's most personal thoughts and experiences, all conveyed in a confessional style.

The author, an Arab nationalist and advocate of social and political change in the Arab world, here concentrates on his own life, placing it before us in order to reveal the "nakedness of the world and relationships." Driven by a boundless yearning for homeland, village, childhood, father, and mother, the author's unconscious takes control. He spontaneously recalls dreams, memories, fantasies, and tales, everything hidden in the collective unconscious, archetypes of individual and nation. He applies a psychic activity that has been oppressed since childhood to present reality through scenes both colorful and dramatic. In the words of 'Abd al-Rahman Munif—himself a leading modern Arab novelist—this novel is "revelation, contemplation and remembrance . . . all written in the blood of the heart."

The novel opens with a flashback. The scene is Kafrun, the author's birthplace. Flocks of cranes cluster in the sky in autumn sky as they prepare for migration to warmer climes. Suddenly the calm scene turns bloody as evil hunters open fire on the innocent birds. Wings shattered, they fall to earth, their white and black feathers scattering over the tops of trees and landing in the river, staining it with blood. The child/author watches in fear and distress as the now-silent cranes await their lingering death.

Barakat identifies himself with the crane, which becomes a symbol of oppressed Arab intellectuals—perpetually circling the globe, uncertain where to land; surrounded by evil forces, yet continuously searching for freedom and salvation for self and nation; seeking solutions to the universal contradictions of extremes—boredom and excitement, joy and sadness, poverty and wealth, love and hate, East and West; and, above all else, searching for the meaning of life and death.

The narrator, who at an early age witnesses the aggression of hunters and the evil of people in general, is thereafter psychologically traumatized by the injustice inflicted on birds, individuals, societies, and nations. Disgusted by the ugliness of the world around him, he advocates revolt, freedom, and revolution in all aspects of the life of individuals and societies. He sincerely believes that Pablo Neruda's verses—quoted on the first page of the novel—apply to the Arab world. Further, he believes that Neruda's vision of the bird applies to Barakat himself as he advocates a vision of salvation.

Barakat tackles many difficult themes, varied in time and place and culled from past, present, and future. He takes it upon himself to lead the Arab world toward salvation by presenting visions of light. For Arab nationalists and penseurs this is neither strange nor new; Arab poets and novelists have long had the task of chronicling the suffering of Palestinians, Arab disunity, and tyrannical leadership. In *The Crane*, Barakat expands this function beyond the Arab world itself, citing hunger and poverty in Africa, the war in Vietnam, racial discrimination in the United States, and the suffering of Japanese children in the wake of Hiroshima's nuclear bomb. He empathizes with the powerlessness of the oppressed. In voicing the concerns and agonies of the voiceless, the idealistic Barakat repeatedly preaches resistance and protest.

The author's account of the shock and pain he felt as a child standing by his father's deathbed is one of the most moving prose passages in modern Arabic narrative. Descriptions of his father's personality pervade the novel; the reader retains the impression of a fascinating paternal figure; a genuine man of olden times, possessed of both dignity and integrity; a family man, devoted to his wife and children, overflowing with love and sacrifice. The description is indeed poignant:

> I can remember that my father motioned to me to sit next to him. . . . Outside, clouds returned to encircle the earth and smother its breath; their dark shadows entered the house and lingered where I sat beside my father. . . . My father's hand reaches out to take mine. He puts it to his lips and kisses it. He draws me toward him and lays his face against mine. . . . Suddenly his hands rise toward the ceiling, then come down again slowly. He grinds his teeth, and I stare at him terrified. In his eyes I see a total change; no doubt, he is staring death in the face. Unable to move, I yell for my mother in a strangled voice.

The child who loses his young father in Kafrun and thus witnesses the sudden and painful death of his ideal and role model, emigrates to America and becomes a professor. In his new country, he is once again confronted by death, this time involving his aged mother. However, the experience is very different. The wonderful woman—someone to whom the author has penned a dedication in one of his previous works ("To the heroine whose life is continuous giving and ceaseless love") is now senile and has other health problems. She has fallen into a coma and hovers between life and death. She is caught between worlds, and the author is trapped there with her. Reliving his father's death and tortured by his mother's pain, he prays to God to take her back, both for her sake and his own. Raising universal questions about the meaning of life and death, the author's poignant portrayal of his saint-like mother creates a powerful and lasting image.

Within the frame of Barakat's psyche nothing ever vanishes, and so he is able to invoke yet another affecting personality from early childhood. The reader encounters Makhul, a mentally handicapped, strange-looking, poor, and homeless creature, who is constantly humiliated by the village children. They all make fun of him because he is abandoned and unwanted. But one evening the author's father sings a lovely melody in his beautiful voice, and the reader is treated to the emotional scene as Makhul weeps while the verses pierce his soul.

Perhaps the greatest service that Barakat has performed in *The Crane* is for Kafrun itself, his birthplace. His devotion to this small town that figures so prominently in the novel is palpable; descriptions of its valleys, orchards, trees, roads, fruits, and community are prominent features of the narrative. Barakat makes of Kafrun a historical place, just as the Iraqi poet, Badr Shakir al-Sayyab, did earlier with a brook named Buwayb—thus turning it into one of the Middle East's most prominent waterways—and with the small village where he was born, Jaykur. As a result of such personal identification, these places have acquired a special kind of emblematic significance in Arabic literature.

While the narrator provides the reader with a rich portrait of most of his major characters, it is interesting to note that his wife (referred to throughout as "the beloved") is somewhat differently, perhaps even less vividly, characterized. The dialogues between husband and wife become a vehicle, a narrative device, whereby their discussions and arguments can be utilized to provoke dreams, invoke past memories, and project thoughts into the future. Throughout the work it is the intellectual partnership of the union that is emphasized rather than the love that lies behind it.

*The Crane* is a novel of great conviction and sensitivity. Its candor and confessional style make it unique. Here is a novel filled with poetry and passionate commitment and resistance. It serves as a mirror of the author's soul, a record of his personal history and that of his village, and, by extension, other "villages" as well. It is like a tree on which have been hung the events of generations. For its author and his accomplishments it is birth certificate and passport. Above all, *The Crane* is a valuable addition to the library of modern Arabic fiction. It transforms our perspective on events and scenes, both familiar and unfamiliar. In the words of the Syrian poet, Shawqi Baghdadi, it "captivates the heart and cleanses the soul."

## Modern Arabic Literature
from the American University in Cairo Press

Said al-Kafrawi *The Hill of Gypsies*
Sahar Khalifeh *The End of Spring*
*The Image, the Icon, and the Covenant* • *The Inheritance*
Edwar al-Kharrat *Rama and the Dragon* • *Stones of Bobello*
Betool Khedairi *Absent*
Mohammed Khudayyir *Basrayatha: Portrait of a City*
Ibrahim al-Koni *Anubis* • *Gold Dust*
Naguib Mahfouz *Adrift on the Nile* • *Akhenaten: Dweller in Truth*
*Arabian Nights and Days* • *Autumn Quail* • *The Beggar*
*The Beginning and the End* • *Cairo Modern*
*The Cairo Trilogy: Palace Walk, Palace of Desire, Sugar Street*
*Children of the Alley* • *The Day the Leader Was Killed*
*The Dreams* • *Dreams of Departure* • *Echoes of an Autobiography*
*The Harafish* • *The Journey of Ibn Fattouma*
*Karnak Café* • *Khufu's Wisdom* • *Life's Wisdom* • *Midaq Alley* • *Miramar*
*Mirrors* • *Morning and Evening Talk* • *Naguib Mahfouz at Sidi Gaber*
*Respected Sir* • *Rhadopis of Nubia* • *The Search*
*The Seventh Heaven* • *Thebes at War* • *The Thief and the Dogs*
*The Time and the Place* • *Voices from the Other World* • *Wedding Song*
Mohamed Makhzangi *Memories of a Meltdown*
Alia Mamdouh *Naphtalene* • *The Loved Ones*
Selim Matar *The Woman of the Flask*
Ibrahim al-Mazini *Ten Again*
Yousef Al-Mohaimeed *Wolves of the Crescent Moon*
Ahlam Mosteghanemi *Chaos of the Senses* • *Memory in the Flesh*
Buthaina Al Nasiri *Final Night*
Ibrahim Nasrallah *Inside the Night*
Haggag Hassan Oddoul *Nights of Musk*
Abd al-Hakim Qasim *Rites of Assent*
Somaya Ramadan *Leaves of Narcissus*
Lenin El-Ramly *In Plain Arabic*
Ghada Samman *The Night of the First Billion*
Rafik Schami *Damascus Nights*
Khairy Shalaby *The Lodging House*
Miral al-Tahawy *Blue Aubergine* • *The Tent*
Bahaa Taher *Love in Exile*
Fuad al-Takarli *The Long Way Back*
Latifa al-Zayyat *The Open Door*